JINGLE BELL ROCK

ELLA FRANK
BROOKE BLAINE

Copyright © 2020 by Ella Frank & Brooke Blaine

www.ellafrank.com

www.brookeblaine.com

Edited by Arran McNicol

Cover Design: By Hang Le

No part of this book may be reproduced in any form or by any electronic or mechanical means, including information storage and retrieval systems, without written permission from the author, except for the use of brief quotations in a book review.

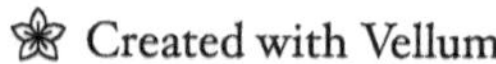 Created with Vellum

Breaking News

Headlines

Sunset Cove Series

Finley

Devil's Kiss

Masters Among Monsters Series

Alasdair

Isadora

Thanos

Standalones

Blind Obsession

Veiled Innocence

PresLocke Series
Co-Authored with Brooke Blaine

Aced

Locked

Wedlocked

Fallen Angel Series
Co-Authored with Brooke Blaine

Halo

Viper

Angel

An Affair In Paris

Lust. Hate. Love

Elite Series

Co-Authored with Brooke Blaine

Danger Zone

Need For Speed

Classified

Co-Authored with Brooke Blaine

Sex Addict

Shiver

Wrapped Up in You

All I Want for Christmas...Is My Sister's Boyfriend

Halo

Viper

Angel

An Affair In Paris

Lust. Hate. Love

Elite Series

Co-Authored with *Ella Frank*

Danger Zone

Need For Speed

Classified

Standalone Novels

Co-Authored with *Ella Frank*

Sex Addict

Shiver

Wrapped Up in You

All I Want for Christmas...Is My Sister's Boyfriend

Dear Reader,

2020. What a shitfest, right?

When we were trying to come up with a Christmas story for this year, nothing felt right. New characters seemed out of reach, and the idea of creating a new world during this difficult time seemed daunting.

What we really wanted was to snuggle up under a cozy blanket with a mug of hot chocolate in hand and some of our favorite friends on our Kindles.

What better way to do that than to create a night that could bring some of our most beloved characters from across the Ella and Brooke universe together?

So this story is for all of our readers, and we hope it makes you feel as happy, nostalgic, and joyful as it does us.

Just think of it like all of our characters giving you a big, warm bear hug.

Merry Christmas and happy holidays from us to you.

Love,
Ella and Brooke

P.S. This story takes place B.C.—"before children." Which means the status of all the couples is wherever they stand when their book or series ends, not counting the epilogues.

ONE

THE SOUND OF "Rockin' Around the Christmas Tree" playing somewhere in the apartment greeted me as I stepped out of the shower, and I chuckled. For someone who claimed he didn't care for holiday music, Solo sure had been listening to Christmas songs on the radio nonstop for two days.

I wrapped a towel around my waist and headed into the living room, and the sight that met my eyes made me grin. Solo sat on the couch with his phone in hand and was listening intently to the radio propped up beside him.

"Starting to feel the holiday spirit, are we? Where did—"

"Shh." Solo held up a finger, never taking his eyes off his phone. As the song faded, an announcer came on, and I could've sworn Solo's ears perked up.

"You're listening to WZLA's holiday channel, and coming up, we've got a special surprise guest in the studio. The one and only Ace Locke is here to give away a pair of VIP tickets to the sold-out Christmas Jingle Ball charity event, and trust me, you're not going to want to miss this. Stay tuned."

As a commercial took over the airwaves, Solo bumped the volume down a notch and finally looked up at me, his eyes sparkling with excitement. "Did you hear that? Ace fucking Locke is giving away the tickets."

"Is this why you've become a man obsessed lately?"

"I'm going to win these tickets. It'll be the perfect way for us to get out of spending the holidays with your folks—no offense." He motioned for me to join him on the couch, and before my ass hit the leather, he kept going. "We can drive up to L.A., stay in a nice hotel, relax, and then—get this—go see Ace Locke, Trent Knox, and...Fallen Angel."

My eyes went wide. "What?"

"Yep. They'll all be there. That's why I have to win these tickets."

I opened my mouth to speak, but couldn't get anything out, because oh my God... Fallen Angel?

Like he could read my thoughts, Solo smirked and nodded. "And not only would we watch the show, these are VIP tickets, meaning—"

"We'd meet them? Holy shit, would we get to meet them?" My heart began to race at the possibility, and I reached across Solo to turn the volume on the radio back up. "You better win those damn tickets."

Solo laughed. "What do you think I've been trying to do?"

"Have I mentioned how much I love you?"

"I haven't won yet."

"Just the fact that you're trying to get tickets to see my favorite bands..." I shook my head. "You're a romantic under all that hotshot bravado, but don't worry. I won't tell anyone."

Solo shot me his secret heartbreaker smile, the one that simultaneously made me weak in the knees and had me shifting on the couch. Before I could even think about making a move, the deejay was back and Solo sat up, his focus intense once again.

"It's the moment you've all been waiting for, and I can't believe it myself, but we've got Hollywood's hottest action star Ace Locke live in the studio with us. Ace, thank you for being here."

"Great to be here," came a deep voice, instantly recognizable to the millions of people who'd watched him on the big screen for years.

"First off, if I don't tell you my wife, Cassie, is your biggest fan then she may not let me come home tonight."

Ace chuckled, low and seductive. "Well, we can't have you sleeping in the street. Is she here?"

"Oh, I made sure she stayed behind that glass over there. For everyone listening, yes, I made my wife stay in another room, because if you saw the way she's looking at him right now, you'd be worried too that she'd jump him given the chance." A few seconds later, the deejay groaned. "And now Ace has gone over to give her a hug... Oh, great. I'm pretty sure she just died happy. I'm now a widower, guys. Awesome."

"Can I just say, your wife smells amazing," Ace said when he got back on.

"Ace Locke, I'd hate to have to kill you."

"Nah, no need. I'm still a happily married man."

"And how *is* Dylan these days? I swear I pass him on ten different billboards on my way to work."

"Lucky you," Ace said, a smile in his voice. "He's great, busy as ever. As a matter of fact, he's at the Lyons arena now doing a shoot while they finish setting up."

"Which is a great lead into why you're here. Tell us about this big event happening tomorrow."

"Well, I think we can all agree it's been one hell of a year, am I right?"

I found myself nodding along with Solo, who still had that intense look of concentration on his face that made me bite back a smile. He wanted this *bad*, and now that I knew what was up for grabs, so did I. With me so often traveling with the Blue Angels, and Solo working on base here at NAFTA, a few days together in L.A. sounded like heaven.

"Many of the nonprofit organizations around the country are struggling to raise funds right now, which means there are more people out there going hungry. There are more LGBT youth on the streets, unable to get the help they need. It means funding for the arts has been slashed. So many out there need our help, so we've put together a fundraiser at the Lyons arena tomorrow night, and we've invited some of the biggest names in entertainment to help us out."

"I've seen the list, and can I just say, the fact that you've got Trent Knox and his old band Fallen Angel co-headlining seems like a massive feat."

Ace chuckled. "It'll definitely be worth the price of admission to see them share the stage, that's for sure."

My eyes grew wide, and Solo jerked his head in my direction.

"Did he say—"

"Sharing the stage...?" I said. "Oh *shit*. Get those damn tickets."

"It sounds like the Christmas Jingle Ball is going to be the can't-miss event of the year," the deejay said. "And you're here to give a lucky fan the chance to be there."

"That's the plan. We've got a couple of VIP tickets up for grabs, which includes meet-and-greets with all the entertainers."

"Yourself included?"

"You know it."

"Well, let's get this thing rolling. Callers, get ready."

I stopped breathing as Solo's finger hovered over the call button, the number to the radio line already typed out on the screen of his cell.

"Ace, what's the lucky number tonight?"

"Let's go with...twenty-four."

"All right, you heard the man. We'll take caller twenty-four starting...now."

Solo hit the call button and cursed. "Busy." I watched as he dialed again and again, until the deejay said, "All right, we've hit the magic number. Caller twenty-four, what's your name and where are you from?"

With a look in his eyes that broke my heart, Solo glanced up at me and shook his head. As he lowered the phone, I reached over to rub his back.

"You tried. It's the thought that counts." I pressed a kiss to his temple and could feel a deep sigh emanating out of him. "Thank you."

Solo opened his mouth to respond, and then frowned, looking over at the radio.

"Caller? Did we lose you?" the deejay said. "Yep, we lost

them. Let's try this again. Caller twenty-four, these VIP tickets are yours."

Without hesitation, Solo dialed the number again, and this time—

"Caller twenty-four, what's your name and where are you from?"

Solo's mouth fell open as he faced me and pointed at the phone. "Mateo Morgan, Mesamir, California. Holy sh—" The rest of his words were bleeped out, and Solo shook his head. "Oh, right. My bad. Holy, uh...crap." I shot him a look, and he shrugged. "What? I can say crap."

Laughter filtered through the speakers, and then the deejay said, "Congratulations, Mateo, you've picked up a pair of VIP tickets courtesy of the man sitting across from me. Say hello to Ace Locke."

For a moment, I wasn't sure Solo was going to say anything at all, which might've been a first in the time I'd known him. The guy had a response for everything, even when you wished he didn't.

I hit his leg. "Say something."

That seemed to knock some sense into him, because then he gave a lazy smile and said, "Ace Locke, how the hell are ya?"

"Doin' well, thanks. Congrats on scoring the tickets. It's gonna be a good time."

"Any idea who you'll be bringing with you?" the deejay asked.

"I guess I'll have to prowl the bars for someone— Ow." Solo rubbed the spot on his arm where I'd punched him. "On second thought, I should probably bring my boyfriend or I'll come home to all my stuff out on the lawn."

"Wise man," the deejay said as Solo stood up and then straddled my lap, a wicked smirk on his face.

"Well, I'm looking forward to having a drink with you guys," Ace said.

Solo ground his hips over mine and nodded. "Oh, we're definitely looking forward to coming." He winked. "Thanks again, Ace."

I couldn't tell if the blood rushing through my veins was because of the fact that we'd be meeting some of the hottest—and biggest—entertainers in the world tomorrow, or if it was courtesy of the man stroking my dick to full mast.

"Mateo, stay on the line and we'll grab your information."

"Sure thing." He leaned in, brushing his lips against mine, and then whispered, "Merry Christmas, Panther."

TWO

LOGAN

"REMIND ME AGAIN why I agreed to this?" I reached for the gin and tonic the bartender had just slid across the counter, then turned to follow Tate to an empty table that overlooked the busy tarmac outside.

It was Friday afternoon, and we were heading out of town for the weekend to some Christmas charity event Ace and Dylan were hosting. He'd called up with two tickets reserved just for us, and unfortunately, the lure of sun over snow had been just the right carrot to dangle in front of my husband. Hence, I was now seated in a bar overlooking a busy runway.

"I hate flying," I said, then took a sip of my drink. "I *especially* hate flying at Christmas. All these people, the rushing around, the Christmas music. It's like they've all forgotten that they have to strap themselves into a four-hundred-ton plane and hope to God it gets off the ground before they can have a very merry anything. It's insanity."

Tate's lips quirked as he picked up the menu on the table between us. "You know, if you ever want to switch careers, I

8

think you'd have a real shot in advertising. You really know how to bring home the Christmas spirit."

"The only spirit I'm interested in right now is the kind that will make me forget what I'm about to do."

"Oh, come on, it won't be that bad. The flight isn't even that long."

"Anything beyond me strapping in and the plane taking off is too long."

"I don't remember you complaining this much the last time we flew."

"That's because we were flying to St. Lucia for our honeymoon, and I knew you'd be naked for a full week straight. That plane could've gone down over the Atlantic and I would've swum the rest of the way to that island."

Tate chuckled. "Hmm, I don't remember the *plane* going down during that trip. You, however..."

My eyes roamed over Tate's leather jacket, burgundy t-shirt, and well-worn jeans, and I had a very vivid flashback of him stretched out beneath the sheer canopy of our island bed, naked as the day he was born.

I took a sip of my drink and tongued my lower lip. "Are you trying to distract me or torture me?"

Tate leaned back in his seat and widened his straddle. *Torture me...tease.*

"I'd settle for either if it stops your freak-out."

"I'm not freaking out. I'm thinking of all the times I'd miss out on seeing you naked if we didn't make it home."

"Oh my God." Tate let out a full-on laugh. "That's a little dramatic, don't you think? You could've told Ace *no* when he offered the tickets."

"I wasn't about to do that. You've been talking about

going somewhere warm for Christmas for years. And *this* is a much shorter trip than Australia."

Tate leaned across the table and took the glass out of my hand. He downed the end of my drink, then took my chin between his fingers. "Remind me to thank you for the sacrifice later."

My eyes lowered to the tempting lips mere inches from mine. "Count on it."

Tate reluctantly let me go and moved back to his seat—safely out of reach. Then he picked up the menu and read it over again. "Let's order. I'm starving. How about the cheeseburger and fries? It'll help soak up the alcohol."

"Sounds good to me."

"Okay, I'll be right back." Tate got to his feet, then stopped. "You're not going to run away, are you?"

I arched an eyebrow. "While my desire to not fly anywhere is strong, my desire to be where you are is much stronger."

A sensual smile slowly stretched across Tate's gorgeous face, and when he leaned down and grazed his lips over mine, his soft curls brushed my cheek. "Go."

He pulled back, and my heart thumped at the love swirling in those dark eyes.

"Going..."

I watched as he took a couple of steps back, and when he turned to head to the bar, I drank in the sight of his long legs eating up the space with a confidence that made my entire body sit up and pay attention.

Damn, my husband was one sexy motherfucker.

I looked out the window and groaned as snow flurries began to fall from the sky, adding that to my list of reasons I didn't like to fly out of Chicago at Christmas. Now, not only did I have to worry about the plane getting off the ground, I was busy imagining it slipping and sliding down the runway. This was great...*juuust* great.

I was about halfway through a ten-point list of reasons why we shouldn't go anywhere this weekend, when my phone buzzed and I saw Ace's name flash up on my screen. Perfect timing. I could let him down easy. Give him a chance to give our tickets to someone who didn't have to risk their lives to use them.

"Well, if it isn't Hollywood's hottest, gayest action hero calling."

Ace's instantly familiar chuckle vibrated through the phone. "And Chicago's most loud-mouthed pain-in-the-ass lawyer answering."

I smirked. "Now, I'd agree with the first half of that statement, but not so much the second half. I'm all about the *pleasure* when it comes to Tate's ass."

I could all but hear Ace's eyes roll as he groaned in my ear. "Thanks for the overshare, as always. But funnily enough, I wasn't calling for an update on your love life. I was calling to make sure you're not plotting ways to avoid getting on the plane. Like getting fall-on-your-ass drunk."

I sat up a little straighter in my seat and looked over my shoulder, wondering how in the hell Ace knew what I was doing. I scanned the low-lit interior, where a brightly decorated tree graced one corner, and tinsel and twinkle lights lined the bar. That was when I saw Tate holding his phone up, grinning at me.

"Tate texted you."

"I have no idea what you're talking about."

I narrowed my eyes on my husband, who clearly knew me well enough to call in reinforcements. "I don't know why you won that award last month for best actor. You can't lie worth a shit."

"And you are totally predictable. Do you really think I needed Tate to text me to know that you were trying to dream up ways not to come out here? It took the bribe of a free stay in Cabo—all expenses paid—to get you to my damn bachelor party."

Tate started back in my direction, a glass in each hand.

"You're lucky there's someone other than you that is really looking forward to this trip."

Ace chuckled. "Uh huh. Tell Tate we'll see him tomorrow. Dylan's looking forward to it. And Logan?"

"What?"

"Have a safe flight."

I opened my mouth, about to tell him not to jinx us, but the smug fucker had already hung up. Really, the guy had access to his very own private jet. Why the hell we were always the ones flying to see him, I had no clue. Next time we got together, he could come back to Chicago.

"Everything okay?" Tate handed me my drink and then moved to take his seat.

"Other than the fact that I have a scheming husband? Yes, I'm just fine."

Tate propped his ankle on his knee and shrugged. "It never hurts to call in reinforcements."

"I see. Well, don't think there won't be repercussions for your little...deception."

Tate's lips tipped up in a wicked-hot smirk. "Oh yeah?"

I slowly lowered my gaze over his relaxed frame and felt

my cock throb at all the delicious ideas that came to mind. "Count on it. I have hours now to think up a suitable punishment. And Tate?"

"Yeah?"

"The first thing you're going to do when we get to our hotel room tonight is grovel at my feet."

Tate's eyes dropped to my lap, and I didn't even bother trying to hide my erection. Then he licked his lips and raised his dark eyes to mine. "Can't fucking wait."

THREE

PRIEST

"ALL RIGHT, OUT with it, you two. You said you'd tell me where we were going once we got to the airport."

Julien and I placed our suitcases by one of the ticket kiosks and looked to our young husband, who was watching us with narrowed eyes. All week Robbie had been employing every trick up his sleeve in an effort to get us to tell him what we had planned for this little surprise getaway, but so far we'd managed to resist.

"No, I said you'd find out once we got to the airport. It's not my fault you haven't worked it out yet."

One of Robbie's perfectly manicured eyebrows rose as he eyed me closely, then he turned his gaze on Julien, who stood close-lipped beside me.

"It is so your fault. The two of you are like Fort Knox. Just when I think I get through one door I bump right into another." Robbie pouted. "I hate it when you two gang up on me."

"Now, now, *princesse*, there's no need to lie," Julien said beside me. "You love it when Joel and I...gang up on you. At least you did this morning, *non?*"

My lips twitched as Robbie crossed his arms and really tried to ramp up his indignation, but he wasn't fooling anyone. We knew our princess all too well, and if there was one thing Robbie loved, it was a surprise—and this one was going to blow his mind.

"That's not what I meant, and you know it." He angled his pointy little chin in Julien's direction. "And trying to distract me with memories of you two all naked and sexy—nope, it won't work."

I chuckled. "Okay, so no talking about how I can't wait to taste that pouty mouth of yours again really soon."

"Not unless you tell me *where* it is you'll be tasting it."

"In that case, I guess we'll just think about it, and you can keep pouting about it."

I went to turn away, and Robbie took my arm, halting me. As we faced off with one another, he took a step forward and moved his hand to my waist. I gave him a pointed look as the handsy minx slowly slid his palm to the back of my jeans, and when his fingers slipped into my pocket, he pulled my wallet free.

"Find out for myself, huh?" Robbie brought my leather billfold up between us and batted his lashes. "Okay. Well...I think our flight confirmation number is on a Post-it note tucked nice and neat in the money compartment here. Just like when we go to the movies."

I narrowed my eyes, and Robbie's smile turned triumphant.

"Aww, and here you thought I was just a pretty face. See, I pay attention."

I wrapped my fingers around Robbie's wrist and pulled him to me so his hand and my wallet were caught between our chests. When he angled his face up toward mine, I ghosted my lips across the top of his, and when he sighed, I grinned and did it again.

"I've never thought you were *just* a pretty face. But you are very pretty."

Robbie rolled his eyes, but the lovely blush on his cheeks belied his projected indifference.

"If you think compliments are going to make me all swoony and forget how stubborn and evasive you two have been the last couple of days—"

"Yes?"

Robbie let out a huff. "Then you just might be right. But can you do it over there. I have a secret to unlock."

I stepped aside and took Julien's hand, as Robbie made his way to the kiosk and fished out the Post-it note he had guessed was in my wallet.

"He's got your number," Julien said as he leaned into my side.

"Hmm." I pressed a kiss to Julien's temple. "I think you might be right."

"Oh, I know I'm right." Julien angled his face up toward mine, and those stunning emerald eyes all but shined. "He almost had you yesterday. If it hadn't been for my well-timed meal, you would've caved like a house of cards, *mon amour*."

"Can you blame me?"

"In that outfit?"

Julien turned his attention to our husband facing the kiosk and ran his eyes down Robbie's tall, lithe frame. From the back, he looked phenomenal. In a body-hugging green sweater and jeans that molded to his tight ass, little was left to the imagination. But when he'd first stepped out of our en suite this morning, his choice of sweaters had left us both... speechless, to say the least.

I let out a low chuckle. "Well, no. I was thinking more about yesterday's outfit. That sweater is—"

"Oh my God. We're going to L.A.?" Robbie spun around with three tickets in his hand, and the smile on his face was almost as bright as the colored lights and silver tinsel decorating his Christmas sweater that read: *Grinch, don't steal my vibe.*

"*Oui, princesse.*" Julien grinned as Robbie practically skipped back to us.

"Which I'm hoping will inspire you to remove that God-awful sweater you're wearing," I said.

Robbie screwed his nose up. "Oh, hush, I'm being festive."

"Is that what you call it?"

"It is. But it doesn't matter anyway. Since you wouldn't tell me where we were going, I dressed for all occasions."

Robbie handed over the tickets to Julien and reached for the hem of his sweater to reveal a fitted red shirt with a huge pine tree in the center. Across the top and bottom, in all caps, was: WHERE DO YOU THINK YOU'RE GOING TO PUT A TREE THAT BIG? And while that was enough to raise an eyebrow or two, I knew our husband well enough to know that there was more to his shirt than that.

I held a finger up and motioned for him to turn, and with a grin full of mischief, Robbie made a slow pirouette showing off—*there it is*—his answer to the question at hand. BEND OVER AND I'LL SHOW YOU.

"*Mon dieu.*" Julien bit down on his lip to hold back his laugh.

Robbie glanced over his shoulder. "What? Do you think it's too obvious?"

"I'd be disappointed if it wasn't."

Robbie gave us a grin, then hiked his carry-on bag up his shoulder. "So...what's in L.A?"

"Palm trees."

"Beaches."

Robbie's frown reappeared. "That's not what I meant, and you know it."

"*Oui*, we do. But that's part of the surprise. Just know that this time our visit is all about fun."

"Fun and *family*," I added.

"We thought it was time to have a do-over." Julien brought Robbie's hand up to his lips and placed a kiss there. "We want to introduce you to the L.A. where we fell in love, *mon cher petit.* The L.A. where we got married. Aaaand we have a few other surprises up our sleeves."

Robbie looked between the two of us, his eyes twinkling much like the lights on the sweater he'd stuffed back into his carry-on. "You two spoil me way too much. You know that, right?"

A smile curved my lips. "Yes."

"Okay, well, as long as you're aware of it, I don't feel guilty for enjoying it as much as I do."

Julien and Robbie started toward the luggage drop-off area, and his laugh filled my ears. As I followed along behind them, I couldn't help but think I was the luckiest man in the world.

FOUR

TATE

"I'M STARTING TO think I should've put you by the window—that way there'd be less chance of you making a break for it."

Logan's fingers tightened around the latest gin and tonic he'd just been given. "If you think for one minute I want to see the ground disappearing out from under me at supersonic speed—*or*, for that matter, hurtling toward us as we plummet to the ground—you're out of your damn mind."

I grinned. "Ah, I see. Would it help if I promise to pull down the shade if that happens so you don't see it coming?"

"I'm glad you find my fear so amusing."

I leaned over and placed a hand on Logan's thigh, the warmth of his skin radiating through his jeans. "I don't find it amusing. But three gin and tonics in and your dire predictions are getting the better of you. Maybe you need a little distraction..."

Logan's striking blue eyes locked on mine as I inched my hand up his thigh.

"A distraction, huh?"

This close to Logan, it was easy to forget I was on a plane that was quickly filling with people, when all I wanted was to lean forward and take his mouth with mine. But knowing that would do nothing but leave us both frustrated for the next handful of hours, I did the next best thing—I teased my husband mercilessly.

I lowered my eyes to Logan's wicked mouth and imagined the way he'd used it on me earlier in the day, the sinful way he'd traced his tongue over every inch of my skin until I demanded he get inside me.

"Fucking hell, Tate. Whatever you're thinking about right now, I want to know."

I slipped my hand down the inside of his leg and squeezed, and a low groan left Logan's lips. "I was thinking about your mouth, and how good it felt on my—"

"Logan? Tate?"

We froze and blinked at one another.

"Oh my God, it is you!"

Logan's jaw clenched as Robbie's voice surrounded us, and as I slowly removed my hand, I grinned. "Well, if that's not enough to distract you, I don't know what is."

Logan took a deep breath in, let it out, then turned to see Robbie had stopped in the aisle beside him, Julien and Priest right on his heels.

"This is crazy," Robbie said as his eyes ping-ponged between the two of us, and then to the three empty seats in the aisle. "What are you doing here? I mean, hello, obviously you're flying to L.A., but what are the odds we're all on the same plane? This is awesome."

"Totally," Logan said in such a droll tone that I couldn't stop my laughter.

As Robbie continued to talk a mile a minute, I read the words on his shirt and then raised my eyes to see Julien and Priest smiling at the two of us.

"This is part of the surprise, *princesse*. Logan and Tate are coming to L.A. with us."

"What?" Robbie's eyes became round as saucers. "Shut the hell up."

Logan mumbled something that sounded a lot like *Yes, please do,* and I bumped him in the shoulder.

"Julien and Priest thought it would be fun to keep it a secret."

Robbie grinned, and when he turned to face his husbands and I read the *back* of his shirt, my mouth fell open. He'd actually walked through the airport in that? Of course he had. I wasn't sure why I was so surprised. This *was* Robbie, after all. The guy didn't have a subtle bone in his body.

Robbie wrapped his arms around Julien's neck and kissed each of his cheeks. "This is going to be the best Christmas ever—"

"So far," Priest said, then started packing their bags in the overhead bins. "Why don't I take the far seat? Julien, you take the middle, and Robbie, how about you sit on the aisle here and help Tate take Logan's mind off the flight."

"Oh, that's right." Robbie crouched beside Logan's seat and patted his arm. "You're scared to fly."

"Not scared." Logan glared over Robbie's head at Priest and mouthed, *I'll get you for this.*

"We could play games," Robbie suggested. "I'm good at

car games, word games. I think I might even have a pack of cards—"

Logan held a hand up. "Do any of those games include alcohol?"

I caught Robbie's eyes from behind Logan's shoulder and shook my head. *He's had enough.*

"Uh...no." Robbie dug around in his carry-on bag and pulled out a bar of chocolate. "But they could involve candy."

"Do you mind if we work out the particulars once we are seated?" Priest looked behind himself at the line gathering.

"Oh, shit, sorry. Let me get out of the way." Robbie moved out of the aisle, perched his ass on Logan's lap, and batted his lashes at me. "Sorry, Tate. This was the only place to move to."

"Uh huh. Sure it was."

"It *was*. Oh, would you look at that, I think Logan's happy to see me."

Logan groaned and turned to glare at me, and I took his drink and downed it in a quick gulp. It was going to be a very long weekend.

Priest arched a brow at Robbie and took his chin between his fingers. "Behave."

"Aww, where's the fun in that?"

"Do you want the rest of your surprise or not?"

Robbie pouted. "Not fair."

"Yet effective all the same."

"Fine, I'll behave." Robbie turned back to face Logan. "Do you know what my surprise is?"

"I do."

"Robert," Priest said.

Robbie's spine stiffened and a flush stained his cheeks,

then he tapped a finger to Logan's nose. "Be thankful I want my surprise more than to torture you."

"So thankful," Logan said, then he looked at me. "You better have a really big fucking surprise waiting for me when we land."

I grinned and leaned in to kiss his cheek. "I have something *extra* big for you."

Robbie's eyes glinted as he waggled his eyebrows at us.

"Okay, you," Logan said. "Your seat is free over there. Go bother *your* husbands."

Robbie patted Logan's cheek and then jumped up off his lap. "Okay. But if you need me, I'll be right over here."

"I'll try to contain myself."

I snorted, and Logan shook his head. "You are far too amused by my suffering right now."

"Nooo." I cradled his cheek and leaned in. Unable to resist the lure of one more taste before we took off, I slipped my tongue between his lips and sank into the delicious taste that was uniquely Logan. "I never enjoy making you suffer."

Logan's eyes darkened as he nipped my lower lip. "Liar. You're the biggest tease I know."

"And you love it." I reached down and tightened the belt over his lap.

"Maybe a little."

"Maybe a whole fucking lot. Now, get through this flight and I promise to tease you a whole lot more the second the door shuts behind us at the hotel tonight."

As the plane taxied toward the runway, Logan threaded his fingers through my hair. "Promise?"

"Do you doubt me?"

He fingered one of my curls. "Not ever."

"Good, because we're going to have a great weekend."

"If we get there."

I grinned against Logan's lips. "I love you."

"I love you too."

"I know. Otherwise you'd never be sitting here about to take off into the sky."

Logan groaned. "Really, Tate? I was just starting to forget where I was."

"Hmm. Let's see if I can help with that."

As the engines fired up and the plane barreled down the runway, I took Logan's lips in a fierce kiss meant to distract him. I must've done a good job, too, because Logan didn't say a damn thing again until the belt sign flicked off, and he offered to...release me. It was a tempting offer, but I decided a good case of frustration would help distract him through the rest of the flight. Also, he was right—I *loved* to tease him.

FIVE

PAIGE

"*P*AIGE? I THINK you need to come deal with this."

I adjusted the microphone on my headset and looked across the arena to where my assistant, Jasmine, was supposed to be covering the soundcheck for Trent Knox and Fallen Angel. "What's the problem?"

"Uh—"

A loud crash cut off her words as something fell over on the stage, and I cursed. "On my way," I said, passing my clipboard off to another member of my event team. "Make sure the catering area is set up for Julien Thornton's arrival tomorrow, and check on the status of the ice rink."

Major events like this were what I was made for, and though nothing ever ran smoothly, today was already one for the books. We'd been working around the clock, but apparently no one else in L.A. seemed to feel the urgency, because every damn delivery had been late, throwing the schedule into chaos. Mercury retrograde was fucking with me. That was the only explanation. But like I'd let a grumpy planet ruin my masterpiece of a party. Hell no. Not on my watch.

I could feel the tension growing the closer I got to the stage, where Viper of Fallen Angel seemed to be facing off against his old bandmate, judging by the scowl on his face and the defensive posturing.

As I approached the stage, Jasmine sidled up beside me.

"I think they might kill each other," she whispered, hugging her chest.

I lifted a brow. "What makes you think that?"

"Are you *fucking* kidding me?" came a roar that echoed around the arena thanks to the live mic positioned in front of Viper. His words seemed to be directed at Trent, who stood on the opposite side of the stage rolling his eyes.

"What's the problem now, Viper?" Trent said, not seeming at all bothered. "Not getting enough attention? Do we need to stop so your ego can be center stage, or can we get this soundcheck done?"

"Hard to do when you fucked with Halo's amp."

"Excuse me?"

"You heard me. If anyone's ego needs to be checked, it's yours."

Trent ripped off his guitar as he started toward Viper, and whoa, buddy, this was gonna get ugly fast. I ran up the stairs to the stage and—probably not the smartest idea—planted myself smack in the middle of Viper and Trent.

"Guys, can we delay this bloodbath by a couple more days? I've got an epic charity event to pull off, and I kind of need you. You know. Alive. Preferably with faces intact."

"This was a shit idea," Viper grumbled, crossing his arms over the strap of his guitar.

Killian, the bassist for Fallen Angel, and usually the voice of reason, rubbed his hand over his face. "What happened to a truce? I thought we'd all cleared the air—"

"You really expect Trent to follow through on anything?" Viper said.

"I swear to God—" Trent started forward again, but lucky me, I blocked him, pushing against his chest with my hand and trying not to notice how built said chest was. Damn.

Behind me, Halo was speaking in a low tone to Viper, trying to calm his boyfriend down, while the other members of Fallen Angel, Slade and Jagger, looked on at the scene with amusement on their faces, like they'd seen this play out before a million times. Now I realized why Trent had walked out on the band and forged his own identity—there was nothing like a clash of egos to make things contentious.

Unfortunately for these guys, I wasn't putting up with that bullshit.

"If anyone is about to give a beat-down here, it's gonna be me, you got that?" I took my time giving each guy a withering look—the one my husband, Dawson, said could make a guy's balls climb up into their body. Useful in times like these.

When no one dared to respond, I continued. "Listen, what I need from you is a couple of songs. A simple collaboration, a handful of minutes to appease the thousands of people paying an insane amount of money to see you come together tomorrow. Surely we don't need to waste time talking about whose dick is bigger."

"No, we don't," Viper said. "We all know it's mine."

"Viper. Jesus." Halo shook his head as Viper smirked.

"Yes, Jesus agrees."

"Seriously don't need to know that," I said, though I filed away a Google search for Viper nudes for later. Research purposes and all. "Go back to your places and let's take it from the top." When the guys all kept standing there exchanging looks, I raised a brow. "Right the fuck now would be fantastic."

Not daring to leave the stage yet, I walked over to Halo's setup at the front, a few feet away from Trent's.

"What's this about an amp?" I asked.

"It's fine. It was just unplugged." Halo adjusted the mic in front of him and shrugged. "Probably an accident."

"Can I count on you to try to keep the peace? Or do I need to hire some seven-feet-tall babysitters to keep you all in check?"

Halo quirked a smile and ran his hand over his signature blond curls. He was such a stark contrast to the rest of the guys, all of whom were dark and moody (and sexy as hell too, but that was beside the point). No wonder Viper called him an angel. He definitely looked like one all lit up under the stage lights. "I'll keep him leashed, how about that?"

"Leash, handcuffs, do what you need to." I headed down the stairs and joined Jasmine.

She leaned in and whispered, "I can't believe you just talked to them like that."

"These guys like a strong hand, trust me."

"A strong hand where?"

I winked. "Exactly."

As the guys tuned their instruments, I checked my watch and ran through the list of immediate things needing my attention once I got these guys off.

Well...in a manner of speaking.

Halo and Trent looked at each other, counting down as Viper glared at the back of Trent's head. Once the song began, I breathed a sigh of relief, though we weren't out of the woods yet. I stayed to watch as Halo and Trent volleyed lyrics back and forth, their voices strong and blending together better than I'd imagined after being at each other's throats. Well, maybe not the two of them, per se, but it was still a matter of opposites attracting, so maybe *that* was what had Viper all fired up. Nothing like good chemistry to make someone throw a shitfit.

As the song came to a close, Jasmine and I began to clap, with the rest of the workers in the arena stopping to join in.

"See that?" I said. "Perfect. So can you all just go to your corners now and do that again tomorrow? And try not to kill or maim each other before then? Thanks so much."

As I backed away from the stage, content to check this incident off my list, a crackle came over my headset and then, "Paige? I need you outside. The ice sculptures are here, and they're not the candy canes you asked for."

"No? What did they send instead? Ice presents? Ice trees?"

"Try ice dicks."

I sighed and grabbed Jasmine's arm, dragging her across the arena with me.

I love my job, I love my job, I love my job.

SIX

THE WARM SUN slipping through the curtains was the first indication that my sleep was coming to an end. But it was the alarm clock hitting nine thirty and the familiar sound of Andy Williams' "It's the Most Wonderful Time of the Year" that really confirmed it.

Not that I was complaining—with Dylan pressed up against my side and his arm and leg thrown across my body as though he were holding me captive, waking up was actually one of my favorite times of the day.

"Wakey wakey, Daydream," I whispered, and pressed a kiss to the top of his head.

Dylan let out a sexy little groan and stretched. "Don't wanna."

"No?"

"Nope."

"But we have guests coming over."

"Don't care." He snuggled into my side, his warm lips kissing their way across my chest. "I was having the most delicious dream about this hotshot movie star, and how I swept him off his feet and into my bed."

I chuckled as Dylan shifted on the mattress, his mouth now making its way up the side of my neck. "That's not how I remember it."

"No?"

"No. But it's your fantasy. You can dream about anything you want."

"Oh, thank God because Jason Momoa looked really amazing in my—"

I tackled Dylan to his back, planting a hand on either side of his head. "You better not be dreaming about any movie star other than the one you're married to."

Sharp teeth scraped along my jaw line, and any idea I'd had about leaving this bed suddenly left my head.

"Fine," Dylan said, his beautiful sea-green eyes twinkling with mischief. "But you better give me something to replace the— *Ahh*."

His delicious sigh did wonders for my ego, not to mention my dick, as I ground my hips over his.

"What was that you were saying?" I brushed my lips over the top of his.

"Nothing..." Dylan slipped his hands under my boxer briefs to grab at my ass. "I was saying nothing."

"I don't know." Dylan pumped his hips up, and when his hard cock rubbed up along mine, I smirked. "Sounded like you were wishing there was someone else in this bed with you."

Dylan shook his head on the pillow, his hair all sexy and mussed from sleep. "Nope. You must've misheard me."

I lowered my head and kissed my way along his jaw to his

ear. "Liar. I know how hot you are for Momoa. All those muscles, that long hair…"

Dylan's fingers tightened on my ass, and he turned his face so we were nose to nose. "And? Don't act like you haven't made me watch every single Captain America movie ten times over for the storyline. I know you're checking out America's ass."

I grinned and slipped my hand under Dylan's hips, then I pulled him up flush against me. "I might be, but America's *finest* ass is right here in my bed. It's also legally mine."

Dylan drew one of his hands from my briefs and ran it up my arm to test my bulging bicep. "And all these muscles are mine to lick, bite, and feel when you get all possessive."

"Is that what I'm doing?"

"Isn't it?"

"Can you blame me?"

I rolled to my back, taking Dylan with me, and when he put his hands to my chest and sat up, I groaned. Okay, Chris Evans had nothing on my Daydream. In a skimpy pair of his Calvins, the longer strands of his highlighted hair had fallen down to cover his eyes as he ran them all over me, and he was biting into his lower lip as though imagining which part of me he was going to taste next.

I smoothed my hands up his muscled thighs and over his hips, and when I slipped my fingers into the elastic of his waistband, Dylan slapped them away.

"What do you think you're doing?" I narrowed my eyes and repeated the move, and this time Dylan took hold of my wrists. "Uh ah. We have guests coming over."

As my earlier words came back to haunt me, Dylan rolled his hips once, twice, and then a torturous third time and pushed up from me, swinging his leg over me to climb off the bed. *Oh hell no.*

"Where do you think you're going?"

"To get ready, of course."

How Dylan managed to sound so serious while he stood there in next to nothing, and an erection that had to be throbbing as hard as my own, was beyond me. "What? You have at least two hours until anyone gets here."

"Exactly. One hour to get the house and food ready, and an hour to get myself ready."

My mouth fell open as I kicked the sheet down my body. "And what about me? You just spent a good ten minutes getting *me* ready. What am I supposed to do with this?"

Dylan grinned like a fiend and backed up toward the en suite. "I'm sure you can think of something."

"You're kidding, right?"

"Sorry, Hotshot, but you're on your own. I have two hours, and anything I start with you would eat into a good portion of that. Come see me after brunch."

"But then we have to get ready for the event." Yes...I was whining.

Dylan's lips twitched as his hand met the handle. "You need a shower?"

Even if I'd been scrubbed down by a hazmat team and scouring brushes, I would've been out of that bed and heading toward the en suite.

"I've never been dirtier in my life."

Dylan pushed open the door and stepped aside. "I sure hope so. Five minutes, tops."

"Make it six, and I don't care if you wanna be top or bottom."

SEVEN

DYLAN

*D*ING DONG!

"ACE? *Ace?* Can you get that?" I took a step back from the table to observe my handiwork and smiled at the festive setup.

A snowy-white tablecloth with a beautiful red and gold runner was draped across our large dining room table, and in the center was a decoration made up of candles, pine cones, and sprigs of holly that would've made Martha Stewart proud.

Christmas music softly filled the house through the insane sound system Ace had installed last year, and as I straightened one of the matching napkins, the doorbell rang again.

"Ace!" I made my way through the main foyer to see Ace jogging down the sweeping staircase.

"I'm here. I'm here," he said as he reached the final step. "They're early."

I glanced at the clock on the far wall and then back to my husband. "No. You're running late."

"I couldn't decide what to wear."

I checked out his final decision and had to admit that the extra minutes he'd spent on his wardrobe was worth it. In perfectly shined Italian leather shoes, grey fitted slacks, and a black shirt tucked in at his trim waist, Ace's broad shoulders and spectacular physique were outlined to perfection. He looked classically handsome, effortlessly sexy, and as I stepped aside for him to walk by, I took in a deep inhale—yep, he smelled like a fantasy too.

About to reach the door handle, I called his name.

"Yeah, Daydream?"

I took in a deep breath and then sighed. "How is it that after all this time you still manage to take my breath away?"

The smile that crossed his lips was one that everyone in the world would recognize. But that special sparkle in his blue eyes? That was all for me.

I sidled in close to him, twined my fingers in his, and pressed a kiss to his lips. "Yep, that's it right there. Did anyone ever tell you that you have a smile worth millions?"

Ace chuckled, and just as he was about to answer me, the doorbell rang...*again*.

"Better get that," I said, squeezing his fingers. "You have an adoring new fan to meet."

"Mhmm. I do."

"And friends to host."

"That too..."

When I just stood there, Ace leaned in and kissed my cheek, then he whispered in my ear, "You look gorgeous, by the way. Make sure your seat is next to mine at brunch."

He pulled back and winked at me, and the full force that was Ace Locke hit me with a one-two punch. I sure hoped the young man coming to meet Ace today had sturdy legs, because holy hell, even now he made my knees weak.

"Deal. Now open the door, Hotshot, before I go out there and tell them to all go home."

Ace grinned and then opened the door wide, and there standing with his finger hovering over the doorbell was Ace's high school buddy—and smart-talking lawyer—Logan Mitchell.

"Well, it's about time you opened the door. I know you're a big shot and you likely need a map to get from point A to point B in this monstrosity, but really, can't you hire someone to answer the door?"

"Logan," Ace said. "I'm so glad to see that you *and* the plane made it in one piece."

"Yeah, yeah. And just so it's crystal clear, next time, you two are coming to us. I'm done flying all over the world to see you like you're important or something."

Ace grinned then turned his attention to Tate. "Has he been like this the whole trip?"

Tate flashed a smile and took hold of Logan's hand. "Only ninety-five percent of it."

Logan looked to his husband and slowly licked his lips. "Yes. The other five percent I've spent accepting Tate's apology for putting me *through* this—over and over again."

Okay, there was the Logan I remembered, unfiltered and one hundred percent inappropriate. A trait that Tate seemed unfazed by, judging by his grin. When a second car headed up the drive, I looked between the two in front of us and said, "It looks like our special guest is here."

Logan glanced over his shoulder, and then back to us. "Special is definitely one way to describe Robbie."

"Logan," Tate said under his breath.

"What? He is...special."

Tate smacked him in the arm and looked to Ace. "What Logan means is that Robbie can be a little bit over the top sometimes."

Ace laughed. "I'm not worried. I've been dealing with all kinds of fans for years."

"And the truth of the matter is," I whispered, "we're extremely curious to meet the two men that the very serious Mr. Priestley ended up marrying."

"That, and Dylan's been panicking about serving food to *the* Julien Thornton."

I slapped Ace's arm.

"Ouch," he said, rubbing his bicep.

"You said you would keep that on the DL."

"Logan and Tate *are* the down-low. I'm not going to tell Julien himself."

I arched a brow at my husband, and when he reached out to smooth a finger over it, I batted his hand away. "Don't try to use your charm on me, mister. Keep it for your new fan."

The car drew to a stop and the door opened up. "Oh my God. This house is like something out of the *Real Housewives of Beverly Hills*."

"He's here," Logan said, and he and Tate stepped aside to reveal three men looking up at the house towering above them.

Two of them I recognized immediately. Joel Priestley, the steely lawyer with the deep auburn hair whom Logan had sent to help us when my horrid (biological) mother had crawled out of the depths of hell to blackmail us. And Julien Thornton, the chef with the jade eyes who'd won *Chef Master*, becoming a household name the minute the camera landed on him.

Not hard to see why. The man was smokin' hot. I mean, his cooking...his *cooking* was smokin' hot.

So that meant the fresh-faced, starry-eyed man standing in the middle of them had to be Robbie.

"You three find the place okay?" Tate finally said. Priestley's lips quirked, Julien's curved, and Robbie's split into a wide grin that practically lit up his face. It was fascinating, as though they were all in sync.

"Did we ever," Robbie said as he hightailed it over to Logan and Tate. He was so wrapped up in his surroundings that he completely missed the two people in his immediate vicinity that he *didn't* recognize. "This place is incredible."

"That it is," Logan said, trying to keep a straight face.

"Does it belong to someone famous? Do you think they do tours with brunch? I'd love to look around. Oh my God, Priest? I bet they have the best bathtub ever here."

"I'm sure they do," Priest said as he stepped up beside his husband—well, one of them. "Why don't you ask them?"

"Huh?" Robbie frowned.

"Why don't you ask them yourself?"

"Myself?" Robbie looked in the direction Priest indicated. "What do you mean ask them my—"

The second his eyes landed on the two of us, Robbie's words came to an abrupt halt and his jaw all but hit the ground.

Yep, there it was, that one-two punch that could only be described as the Ace Locke Effect.

EIGHT

ROBBIE

OH. MY. GOD. *That's Ace Locke.* The *Ace Locke. As in* The Last Guttersnipe, Original Bourbon, *and, hello,* Hard Throttle.

No. No. There was no way Priest and Julien would bring me to meet *the* Ace Locke without telling me. There was no way they wouldn't prepare me for something so... so...monumental.

They knew how I was. That I'd want to wear my best clothes, have my hair styled perfectly, have my lips all glossy with my favorite brand of lip gloss, so when I stood in front of Ace smiling stupidly—*like I'm definitely doing now*—I knew that my lips looked totally kissable. Not that I planned to kiss him.

There was no way my husbands would do that to—

"Good morning, you must be Robbie."

—me.

Holy shit. Ace Locke is standing right there. No. He's actually coming closer. He's...he's talking to me. He even said my name...

40

"Princesse?" Julien said softly as he stepped up alongside me. "Are you okay?"

Am I okay? Umm…if one counted the fact that I couldn't seem to get any of the words in my head out of my mouth, okay, then sure, I was doing great. But I might've forgotten how to move my feet.

"Don't mind him," Priest said as he walked past me to shake Ace's hand. "I think he's a little bit starstruck. We didn't tell him we were coming, so he's finding out in real time."

Ace flashed a megawatt grin my way, and I blinked several times. It was surreal, standing within touching distance of someone that was usually on your television or, you know, a fifty-three foot-IMAX screen.

"That's no problem at all. Take all the time you need. We even have alcohol inside."

Oh thank God.

"In the meantime, let me introduce my husband, Dylan."

Uh, no introduction necessary. Any gay man worth his tiara knew Dylan Prescott. Not only did he manage to snag Hollywood's hottest action hero, he was also the face *and* body of some of the sexiest ad campaigns out there.

From Calvin Klein to Giorgio Armani, the man had been plastered on billboards and gracing commercials from the moment his stunning face—and six-pack—had come into view.

"It's so wonderful to see you again, Joel." Dylan reached out and gave Priest a hug, and as I watched the scene from my hiding spot behind Julien's shoulder, I noticed Priest's expression soften. He really liked these two; he didn't soften up for anyone.

"I'm happy to be here. We all are. Thank you again for the invitation."

"Oh, it's our pleasure. It was a great excuse to see you again. Not to mention meet the men in your life."

Priest glanced our way, and his expression shifted from soft to possessive. It was subtle, but the eyes, those stormy grey eyes, never lied. "And I'm pleased to introduce them. Ace, Dylan, my husbands. Robbie, the unusually shy one, and Julien."

When both Ace and Dylan looked in our direction, my breath caught at the sheer beauty of them. It was like something out of a movie.

"*Bonjour.*" Julien, charming and suave as always, stepped forward to greet both men, which left me a mute onlooker.

It was so weird. I was never stuck for words, never this shy, but when Ace glanced my way and winked, my breath got caught and I took great interest in the fact that I wished I had worn my pink leather loafers, not these boring beige ones.

"I've got to say, I might pay Ace to come hang out at the Popped Cherry if it renders you mute for a night."

Logan.

It was a rare day that anyone could take the spotlight off Logan Mitchell, but today was that day. I glared over my shoulder to see him and Tate grinning at me like fools and mouthed, *Shut up.* They started to laugh. Idiots.

"Why don't you come inside?" Ace suggested, and gestured to the open door. "Maybe after brunch I could give you a tour, Robbie."

Priest and Julien were both looking at me, and I could

feel my face flush from Ace's use of my name. But when Logan and Tate laughed even harder at my freak-out, something inside me clicked.

Right, that was it. I was standing in front of Ace friggin' Locke, and was about to walk inside his house and have brunch with him and his hot husband, for God's sake. *Pull it together, Robbie.*

I tilted my chin up, straightened my shoulders, and stepped up to our famous hosts for the morning, then I graced them both with my most winning smile, trying for some of my usual pizazz.

"There's nothing I'd enjoy more than *coming* inside your house." Then I gave a flirty wink to my husbands and decided to let them do with that whatever they wanted to. After all, this was their own fault.

"Funny," Dylan said as he hooked his arm through my elbow and guided me through the open door. "I said something just like that to Ace the first night *I* showed up at this place."

"You did?" I asked, feeling an instant sense of camaraderie with Dylan.

"I did. Up in his bedroom, I believe."

"The first *night?*"

"Mhmm. It was his birthday party, there were hundreds of people, including my own date—"

"Dylan..." Ace said in warning, much like Priest had with me. But luckily, Dylan and I were becoming fast friends—he ignored his husband. Good man.

"What? It's true," he said as he led me through an enormous foyer and past a sweeping staircase.

My eyes widened as we entered a dining room fit for the Christmas issue of *O, the Oprah* magazine. "This place looks amazing."

"I'm glad you think so." Dylan walked me around to a seat by the one at the head of the table. "This is you."

I thanked him and watched as he gestured for Julien and Priest to take the two seats beside me. Logan was at the other end of the table—*thank God*—and Tate and Dylan took the seats opposite us.

That meant that—

"You don't mind if I sit here, do you?"

—*Ace* was sitting right next to me. As in, our feet could touch under the table. Not that I was about to play footsie with him. He was a married man. *I* was married twice over. But seriously, Ace Locke was sitting next to me.

"Would you like a drink, Robbie?"

I glanced up guiltily to find Dylan looking at me, and nodded. "Yes. God yes. The stronger the better."

He chuckled and glanced around the rest of the table, and after everyone was taken care of, he disappeared through a set of doors I assumed led to the kitchen. Not a second later, a young man came out with a tray of mimosas. Mine didn't even have a chance to touch the tablecloth before I took a long gulp of the drink as a loud bang came from behind the doors.

We all looked toward them, and then Julien said, "Uh, should I go and help him, maybe?"

"No way." Ace chuckled. "He's been looking forward to serving *you* all day. If you go in there, he might drop the breakfast tarts on the floor. But don't tell him I told you that."

Ah, so it seemed I wasn't the only nervous one in the midst today. I wondered if Dylan was in there guzzling down his own mimosa.

"My lips are sealed," Julien promised, and that made me look at my husband's fabulous mouth, because wow, Julien really did have the most suckable—

"So, Robbie, are you excited about the Jingle Ball tonight?"

I turned to find Ace's piercing blue eyes locked on mine. As I stared into a face I had seen a hundred times over but never actually *seen*, I said, "You're Ace Locke."

A low rumble of laughter left his throat. "Yes, I am."

"Wow." I quickly took another sip of my drink and this time let my eyes rove all over his famous face.

"And you're Robbie Thornton-Priestley."

I nodded. "Yes, I am."

"That's..." Ace's eyes shifted past my shoulder to my husbands, then came back to mine. "Wow."

A burst of laughter escaped me before I could help it, and wouldn't you know it, Ace's cheeks flushed red.

"I'm sorry, that was rude."

I immediately reached out to assure him it was fine, and the second I squeezed his forearm, I remembered exactly whom I was touching and quickly withdrew.

"Shit. Sorry. I didn't mean to just...touch you."

"You didn't?"

When I just sat there mute, Ace chuckled.

"I mean, Joel told me that I was your freebie, so I just assumed that—"

I whipped around in my seat and pinned Priest with narrowed eyes. "You *told* him he was my freebie?"

Not perturbed in the slightest, Priest brought his drink to his lips and took a sip. "I did."

"Are you *insane?* That's Ace Locke."

Julien was doing his level best not to laugh, as Priest glanced past me and then nodded. "Yes, I believe we established that."

I leaned across Julien and said, "You don't tell someone like him that he's my freebie."

"Why not? This way, he knows what a *big* fan you are."

"I'm going to kill you."

The flame that entered Priest's eyes made my cock instantly respond. "I look forward to it, sweetheart."

I swallowed back the desire I had to grab my infuriating husband and kiss his smug lips, and instead tried for some level of composure.

The look of mischief in Ace's eyes told me he was well aware he was part of a larger plot here, and when I scanned the table to see all attention was on me, I threw back the last of my drink and glared at them all.

"So do we do this here, or do you take me back to your room? Are the others invited? Ooh, maybe Dylan? I mean, I do my best work when I'm in the middle."

Before I could get to my feet to take advantage of Ace's offer—real or not—Logan put in his two cents.

"Jesus, Robbie. Why don't you just strip naked and throw yourself on his lap?"

I shot Tate's bitter half a glare. "Don't be jealous. You and Tate had your chance." Then I turned back to Ace, who still had an amused look on his face. "If you need another option, I look delicious lying across the table—"

"Aaand that's enough, *princesse*," Julien said, draping his arm around the back of my chair to hug me in close.

"Seriously? You're going to deny me the pleasure of *Beckett Sinclair*?" When Julien's brow furrowed—he clearly did not get the reference to one of Ace's hottest characters—I let out an exaggerated sigh. "Come on, I've made you watch it a million times. The one where Ace spends practically the entire movie shirtless."

"Okay, Robert. You've had your fun."

Priest's voice should've been warning enough, but I was on a roll now, and I felt Ace had it coming at this stage. After all, he'd been in on it this whole time. With the champagne from my mimosa nicely singing through my system, I placed an elbow on the table and leaned over to trail my fingertip in a lazy circle over Ace's arm.

"So whaddya say, *Beckett*, want to show me how well you can handle another man's...gun?" I batted my lashes for extra emphasis, and when Ace let out a booming laugh and shook his head, I grinned. "Or maybe you could just sign my—"

"Okay, Robert. That's enough." Priest got to his feet, and I turned to look up at him.

"What? I'm just making sure I make the most of this opportunity. You *do* want me to make the most of it, don't you?"

"What I *want* right now is not polite to do in front of company." Priest's jaw twitched, and the immense satisfaction I derived from my little bout of payback was quite satisfying. Not as satisfying as what I was sure his brand of punishment would be, buuuut this would do rather nicely.

I was just about to tell him that he'd have to wait until

later, when the kitchen door swung open and Dylan stepped through with a tray of breakfast tarts. All heads turned his way, and as he looked over the now-silent table, he smiled brightly and said, "Right, what'd I miss?"

NINE

TRENT

"IS THAT EVERYTHING?"

When I nodded, Shaw zipped the bag I'd be taking to the Jingle Ball event later and set it by the door. Standing at an imposing six-five, and with muscles for days, Shaw Jennings looked more like my bodyguard than my boyfriend, but that wasn't the only reason he got stares wherever we went. The man was damn gorgeous. The first time I'd walked into his tattoo studio, I'd lost my words—and who wouldn't, with those dark brown eyes made for falling into, and the way his tailored clothes molded to his body so perfectly? I trailed my eyes down his body over the white collared shirt he wore paired with black slacks. There was something about the way he kept the top buttons undone and rolled his sleeves up his thickly muscled forearms that always sent a shot of lust straight to my cock.

He smirked. "I know that look, Trent."

"Oh yeah?" I started toward him. "And what's it telling you?"

"That someone is in a dangerous mood."

"And that's a problem?"

"Only when our car service is scheduled to be here any minute."

I moved closer, backing Shaw up against the door, and his eyes sparked. Oh, he wanted it, our schedule be damned. I fingered the opening of his shirt, and the heat of his skin was scorching. I'd kissed those tattoos rising up his neck so many times, but it was never enough.

The second my lips hit his collarbone, Shaw sucked in a breath, his hands moving to my hips to hold me close.

This was exactly what I needed to take the edge off before tonight's show. I'd just lose myself in my man's body and—

Knock, knock, knock.

—answer the fucking door.

I groaned and pulled myself off Shaw, but not before stealing one last kiss.

"What the hell do you want?" I said as I opened the door a crack, only to see Killian standing there, hands shoved in his jeans pockets. "Oh. Hey, man."

He lifted a brow. "Bad time?"

Shaw squeezed my ass, and when I glanced over my shoulder at him, he smirked. *Damn troublemaker.* "Course not. Come on in."

I opened the door and moved out of the way, and as Killian entered the suite, he got a good look at the front of Shaw's tented pants.

"Shit. Sorry to interrupt."

I snorted. "No, you're not."

Killian held back a grin. "Yeah, you're right. I'm not. But

this won't take long."

"I'll go check on the car—" Shaw started, but Killian shook his head.

"Actually, I'd like to speak to you both."

"Oh." Shaw looked at me, and when I shrugged, he gestured toward the couches. "Have a seat."

Always the most chill guy in any room, Killian swaggered into the suite and dropped down into one of the leather chairs. Other than yesterday's soundcheck, I hadn't seen him in a while, but not much had seemed to change since our TBD touring days. He wore his dark brown hair a bit longer now, not the close-cropped 'do he used to sport, and from what I'd heard, he was a one-man guy now, no longer entertaining groupies on a nightly basis. But he was still Killian, the only member of my former life who'd bothered to reach out after I left, so whatever he wanted to say, I'd hear him out.

Shaw and I sat on the couch across from him, and I rested my forearms on my knees.

"So, what can we do for you, Kill?" I said.

He didn't answer right away, only narrowed his eyes slightly as he looked between the two of us. Then a grin slowly lifted his lips. "You two secretly married yet?"

I blinked. "What?"

"Engaged? Living together?"

"The hell are you talking about?"

"I would've figured you'd jump right on that." Killian's smile grew, and he winked in Shaw's direction.

I rubbed my hand over my face. "Is that what you cock-blocked us for? To ask if we're still together?"

"Just wondering if I'd get an invite to the wedding, that's

all."

Shifting back on the couch, I looked at Shaw stretching out his long legs, crossing them at the ankles. He didn't look half as uncomfortable with this topic as I did—not that the idea of being tied to Shaw in any way wasn't something I already thought about on a daily basis. It was more a matter of when than if.

"You think after the shitshow that was yesterday's soundcheck that I'd invite any of you assholes? What the hell was that?"

Killian lifted his hands. "I know. That's why I'm here. To apologize."

"You're not the one who needs to."

"True. But Viper's not...in the right headspace to do that right now."

"Oh, give me a fuckin' break."

"It's true—"

"You're seriously gonna defend him? Again?" I shook my head. "Of course you are, because that's what you do. You play peacemaker and cover his ass, not that he deserves it. Same old story."

"Trust me, I know as well as you do that he can be a dick when he wants to be, but he's changed—"

"Really?" I sat back and crossed my arms. "You know, I thought he'd changed too. I thought we'd truced it out and moved on, which is the only reason I even considered coming out here. But I was wrong."

"No, you weren't. He's just got some shit on his mind, and he's lashing out. You know how he gets."

"Yeah, I do. That's why I left."

"Trent, come on, man. It's not personal."

I jerked forward, a response on the tip of my tongue until Shaw reached over and laid his hand on my thigh. Just one touch from him instantly calmed me down, and I let out a heavy breath.

"Fine. I'll listen. But at least tell me why Viper can't seem to apologize for himself."

"I think he will. Eventually. He's just got...a lot going on today. I can't give you more than that, but trust me, you'd be in the same damn headspace. So just...try to give him a break, yeah?"

I stared down my old bandmate, trying to read between the lines of what he was telling me and why I should give a fuck. Of course I wanted this whole thing to work out. It had to. One of the big selling points for the event was to see us all on stage together like we hadn't had the biggest falling out in rock history. God knew I was the one who got the flack for leaving the band in the first place, and I wasn't about to screw things up now.

"He can do that," Shaw said, squeezing my thigh, and as I looked at him, a small, knowing smile played on his lips. "Right, Knox?"

"You asking me to be the bigger man?" I teased, and when he nodded, I sighed and faced Killian again. "Yeah, fine. I'll try to refrain from knocking him over the head with my guitar."

"That's all I can ask for," Killian said, grinning broadly. "Thanks, man. And just so you know, we're all glad to be doin' this with you. Like old times, right?"

"Yeah." I relaxed back against Shaw's arm, my annoyance and adrenaline draining out of me—for the moment. "Something like that."

TEN

RYLEIGH

"HEY, YOU. DIRTY Dick Dawson. Get over here and tell me what you think of this."

Dawson looked up from where he'd been overseeing the hanging of my *Licked After Dark* banner and, when he saw the shot glasses set out in front of me, quickly moved in my direction.

Thank God Paige had volunteered her husband to be my —in her words—"bitch" for the day, because I wasn't sure I could do this without him. I needed a taste tester who could handle his alcohol as I did a final check of the specialty drinks I'd designed for the Jingle Ball tonight, and since my boyfriend, Hunter, was busy on a construction job, Dirty Dick would have to do.

As Dawson stopped opposite the bar from me, he gave me a lazy grin. Even after all the drinks I'd given him so far, he wasn't glassy-eyed in the least. Things to be grateful for: my BFF and her man being complete lushes.

"More naughty Christmas shots just for me? Are you and Paige trying to get me drunk?"

"She volunteered you for a reason," I said with a wink. "Okay, so I need you to tell me which of these you like the most."

Dawson eyed the three shot glasses filled with varying shades of green mixed liquor. "All of them."

"You haven't even tried them yet."

"But you don't know how to make a bad drink, Ryleigh."

I shook my head. "I appreciate you blowing smoke up my ass, but how about you take the shots, please and thank you."

"Don't have to ask me twice." Dawson lifted the lightest-colored glass to his lips, took a sip, and then made his way down the line.

When he set down the last shot glass, I drummed my fingers along the bar. "So?"

"So I was right. They're all fucking delicious."

"But if you had a favorite, it would be...?"

"All of them."

Groaning, I dropped my head in my hands. "If you don't stop being difficult, I swear I'll have Paige replace your guyliner with a Sharpie."

"Ouch. That's harsh, Ry."

"Then give me an answer so I can finish getting things ready. I only need one Grinch's Jingle Balls."

Dawson stared at me for a beat and then shook his head. "Of course you do. Let me try them again." This time he sipped from darkest to lightest before pushing the middle glass forward. "This one tastes most like a Grinch's Jingle Ball."

"Balls. And about time," I said, grabbing the chalk so I could write the drink's ingredients on the board.

"Is he being difficult? Should I fire him?" Paige's voice rang out as she sauntered toward the bar.

"Mmm, hello, love." Dawson wrapped his arms around Paige's waist and lowered his head to kiss her neck. "You taste even better than a Grinch's Jingle Balls."

Over his shoulder, Paige raised an eyebrow at me. "That hardly sounds like a compliment."

"Oh, but it is." I brushed my chalky fingers on my frilly fifties-inspired Christmas apron and pushed the shot glass her way. "Try it."

She slapped Dawson's ass before pushing him away, and after downing the rest of the green liquor in one swallow, she nodded. "Tasty balls. What else ya got?"

"Well, Ace requested a lemon drop, so that's the Locke Licker. Randy Rudolph is a twist on a cosmopolitan, and we can't forget our favorite white Russian, known today as Santa's Coming."

"Ooh, dirty girl. I like it. Make sure you save me at least three of those for later."

"Locked and loaded, and I'll even put cherries on top."

Paige grinned. "You're so good to me. What would I do without you?"

"Ask Shayne or Quinn to do it?" When she laughed, I knew I had her number. There wasn't anything any one of us wouldn't do for each other, and keeping each other liquored up as needed was the least of it.

"Ugh, I can't believe Quinn's gone MIA, and what the hell with Shayne letting Nate drag her off to freezing Michigan for the holidays? All she'll get there is a pair of blue balls for Christmas." Paige leaned on the bar, her chin resting on her fist. "You know she didn't even have the right clothes? I had to loan her my winter wardrobe."

I shrugged. "It's not like we need heavy jackets in L.A. I'm sure she's fine."

"You're going to give me the 'she's got Nate to keep her warm' spiel now, aren't you?"

"Well, she does. And he *is* pretty hot."

"But she'd have so much more fun *here*. I mean, look at this place." She gestured around at the decorated arena that, even unlit, took my breath away. In a few short hours, this place would be a winter wonderland, and I couldn't wait.

"You've seriously outdone yourself." I noticed Dawson eyeing the remaining shots and pushed the glasses his way before turning my attention back to Paige. "You dying yet?"

"Me?" Paige tossed her long blond hair over her shoulder. "Please. I could do this in my sleep."

"Yeah? I heard some rumblings that the Fallen Angel guys were having issues yesterday."

"Oh, I smacked that shit down real fast. It was more of Viper having an issue with Trent, blah blah blah, ego stuff, blah blah blah, you left the band, blah blah blah, I still hate your guts."

"Uh, they *are* still playing tonight, right?" I couldn't imagine the event could happen without the main performers, and I definitely didn't envy Paige's job. I'd stick to my boozy shakes and drinks, spank you.

Paige rolled her eyes. "Duh. I regulated."

"What my girl does best," Dawson said, throwing his arm around Paige's shoulders and kissing the top of her head, and as she leaned into him, she nodded.

"Damn right. That's what I do—" Paige's words cut off as behind the happy—if not somewhat unconventional—couple, one of JULIEN's catering staff timidly tapped Dawson on the shoulder.

"Excuse me," the girl said, her pale skin blushing fiercely. "I don't mean to bother you, but, um...could I get an autograph?"

The three of us went still, and then, one by one, we looked at each other in confusion.

"I-it is you, right?" the girl stammered, and bit her lip. "From Fallen Angel?"

My snort caught the girl's attention, but I quickly covered up my laugh by coughing. She thought *Dawson* was one of the Fallen Angel guys?

Dawson blinked in surprise, and then he smiled, the cocky, self-assured smile of someone who really *was* a member of one of the hottest rock bands in the world. He dropped his arm from Paige's shoulders and took the girl's hand in his, bending down to press a kiss to her knuckles. "And who do I have the pleasure of meeting?"

Paige looked over her shoulder at me and mouthed, *Is he freaking kidding?* and I had to bite down on the inside of my cheek to keep from laughing.

A dreamy look crossed the girl's face as he took the pen she offered and signed an event brochure, and I had to wonder where she got the idea he was famous. Maybe it was the way he dressed? He was more casual today than usual, but only because he couldn't hang a banner while wearing a suit. But with his long dirty-blond hair, a collared shirt with a gaggle of necklaces holding it open, and rings on most of his fingers—along with the aforementioned guyliner—I guessed he did look like someone who belonged in a band. Too bad I'd heard him sing karaoke, or maybe I'd fall for it too.

Dawson grinned as the girl skipped away, practically walking on air, and Paige groaned.

"Fuck me. There goes his ego boost for the rest of the year. He won't be able to fit his head through our front door."

"Don't be jealous, love. She couldn't possibly have enough issues to keep me completely occupied." His teasing smile was infectious, and I laughed as Paige pushed him back toward the banner that still needed finishing.

"So, Ry. You need more time with your booze, or can you come steal some of JULIEN's gold-dusted truffle popcorn?"

ELEVEN

HALO

"I DON'T THINK we're allowed in there." I stopped just outside the open doors of the conference room that had been converted into a war room for the company putting on the event, and stared at the other four members of my band, who were peering inside like a bunch of busybodies.

Viper—my boyfriend, and also the sexiest guitarist on the face of the planet—glanced over his shoulder with a smirk. "What are they gonna do? Fire us? We're the headliners, Angel. They need us."

It was an arrogant claim, but that was part of Viper's appeal. His confidence. He also wasn't wrong. Ever since we'd arrived at the arena for this weekend's charity ball, Paige and her crew had all but bent over backward to accommodate us. They'd also put up with some rather...contentious rehearsals.

I was still trying to work out *what* exactly had happened yesterday during the soundcheck to make Viper so disagreeable. I'd thought he and Trent had buried the hatchet months ago, but apparently I was wrong. Viper hadn't seemed to relax until the two of us got back to our hotel room, where he told me everything was fine.

So far, that seemed to be the case. He'd woken me up to breakfast in bed, followed by a particularly enjoyable exercise routine that also...took place in bed. Then we'd made our way over here to meet up with the rest of the guys.

"Let's sneak in," Slade, our drummer, suggested. "Find the auction list and check out what's up for grabs."

I frowned and checked to see if there was anyone who looked like they had the authority to grant us entry, but there was no one but us standing in the near vicinity.

"Just like that? Don't you think it would be easier to, I don't know, ask someone if we're allowed in there?"

"Angel..." Viper sauntered over to me, his jeans fitting his legs in a way that was indecent. My eyes roved up to his face, and he ran a hand through his dark hair. "Stop worrying. If someone catches us, I'll tell them it was my idea. That I made you do it."

I scoffed as he hooked his fingers through the belt loops of my jeans and tugged me forward. Then I wrapped my arms around his neck. "Made me, huh?"

"Yep." Viper nipped at my lower lip. "We'll say I blackmailed you."

"Oh yeah? With what?"

Viper's eyes darkened, and wow, as always, everything else around us seemed to vanish. "Hmm. I threatened to sleep on the couch."

That made me laugh. "You would never."

"They don't know that."

Bullshit. Anyone with half a brain would know that Viper would never sleep on a couch if he had a naked body—*my* naked body—in his bed. No way. Viper slept curled around me, connected head to toe, every night of the damn week. "Okay, you win. I'll help you look for the list."

His wicked smile went hand in hand with the arrogance from seconds ago.

"Are you two done?"

I pulled away from Viper to look at Slade, who was watching us with a bored expression.

"We only have a limited time here. Can you suck face later?"

Viper pulled away from me to flip him off. "You're just jealous because Imogen couldn't be here this weekend. I still don't understand why you and Jagger don't just—"

"Halo, muzzle your man, would you?" Jagger said as he glared Viper's way.

"But your partner just told us to stop sucking face." Viper slung his arm around my shoulders. "So which is it?"

"How about you all shut the hell up so we can get in and out of there while no one's watching?" Killian said.

I grinned. "You mean while Levi's busy talking to Paige?"

"Well, yeah. I want to get laid tonight, not spend my time explaining why I snuck in here with you morons."

"Yeah, okay," Slade grumbled. "Don't even try to act like you don't wanna see what's up for grabs."

"I didn't say *that.*"

Killian, Jagger, and Slade walked through the door ahead of us. Viper took my hand and winked at me.

"So, you think there's anything on the list that you want to bid on?"

"Hmm." I pondered his question as he led me into the empty room. "I don't know, you think there might be a date with Ace up for grabs?"

Viper stopped dead in his tracks, and when I looked at him, he scowled. "You better be fucking joking."

I shrugged. "I mean, it *is* Ace Locke."

"He is also *married*. Or have you conveniently forgotten about that?"

Aww, poor Viper—I really shouldn't tease him. But there was something so damn hot about the way he got all possessive over me. "No, I haven't forgotten."

"So you just don't care? What about his husband?"

I frowned, Viper's outrage on this stranger's—Dylan Prescott's—behalf making me chuckle. Of course I cared. I wasn't a homewrecker. I also loved Viper with all my heart. But seeing him all riled up over this was slightly amusing, considering he'd been Mr. Playboy when we first met.

"Well, maybe his husband could come along too."

When I waggled my brows, Viper growled and leaned in to press a hard kiss on my lips. Not a second later, Killian called out, "Found it!"

We pulled apart and hurried over to where the others stood. As he flipped through the pages on the clipboard, Killian let out a low whistle. "Damn, okay, there are some pretty kickass prizes on here."

"Oh yeah? Like what?" Slade looked over Killian's shoulder. Killian quickly moved out of the way. "Hey, no fair. Tell us."

"I found it. I'm looking first."

"It's not like he can bid now, Slade. Relax." Viper smirked

in Killian's direction. "We *all* get to see the list, and then, well, let the best man win."

"Whatever," Killian said. "Hmm, yep, there's one or two things on here I think I'm gonna bid on."

"Okay that's it, hand it over." Jagger grabbed the clipboard out of his hand and flipped through the pages as Slade stood beside him. When they came to the very last one, their eyes widened.

"Holy shit," they said in unison.

"Oh God," Viper said beside me. "Is it a date with Ace fucking Locke?"

"No." Slade shook his head. "Even better, a walk-on spot in one of his movies."

"Shut the hell up."

Yes, that was my boyfriend. You know, the *I'm a kickass rock star* guy? It seemed the possibility of being in a movie with Ace Locke made him more excited than he wanted to admit.

"It's right here, man, look." Jagger handed over the clipboard, and sure enough, there it was. A chance at a walk-on scene with Ace friggin' Locke.

Holy shit was right.

"Damn." I let out a whistle. "That's a hell of a prize."

Viper looked at me and immediately tried for an air of indifference. "I mean, it'd be cool, but—"

"Oh, quit it." I chuckled. "You want that prize as much as we all do."

"Well, I definitely don't want the signed guitar from Trent Knox."

We all laughed, and I gestured for the clipboard. "What else is on there?"

As I flipped through, I saw that along with the prizes we'd already drooled over, there was an Audemars Piguet watch from Dylan Prescott's last campaign up for grabs and a free matchmaking service for a lucky single out there wanting to find love.

"Wait," Slade said, looking over at me. "I didn't see anything from us on there. We donated something, right?"

"Of course we did," Killian said, and then he cut a sly smile in Viper's direction.

"Yeah, we told Paige last night when you went to dinner," Viper added.

"You did?" Slade frowned as he looked between all of us, but I was staying all the way out of this.

"Yep." Killian crossed his arms over his chest. "We told her to put us down for a dare. We're rockers—we wanted to prove we were up to do anything for charity."

Viper grinned like a fiend. "So we put down that they could shave your mohawk off."

Slade's eyes bugged wide. "You did what?"

I looked to Jagger, who was biting back his laugh as Viper nodded. "I mean, you can rock bald for a while, right?"

Slade's eyes darted around all four of us. "You've all lost your fucking minds."

Killian smirked. "But it's for charity."

With a final *fuck you* glare in his direction, Slade turned on the heel of his black boots and stormed out of the room, leaving us laughing behind him.

Viper dropped the clipboard onto the table where we'd found it, and as we left the same way Slade had just gone, Killian said, "How long do you think it'll take him to work out we're fucking with him?"

Jagger shook his head. "Right up until the moment they read out what we *really* offered for the auction."

"Poor bastard," Viper said, though he didn't sound contrite at all. The three of us chuckled and headed out to find our dressing rooms for the night.

SOLO

"I DIDN'T REALIZE limo service was included in the prize," Panther said, sliding his hand up my thigh as his lips met my neck. "Maybe we could have the driver ride around for a while longer."

I moaned and shifted on the leather seat, careful not to spill the glass of champagne we'd been offered when the limo pulled up to our hotel. I would've preferred a Corona, or almost anything else, but I wasn't going to turn my nose up at the bubbly. It was time to relax, and I was going to make sure this weekend in L.A. was nothing but perfect for Panther. Though if he didn't stop trying to rile up my dick, I couldn't promise he'd get all that I had planned.

"So you're saying fuck the show..." I said, catching his hand just as it made its way between my jean-clad thighs. "And the meet-and-greet—"

Panther's mouth stilled on my neck. "Can't it be fuck, then the show?"

I chuckled, not about to complain, but as I let go of his

hand and reached for his neck to steal a kiss, the driver came over the intercom.

"Arrival at the arena is in two minutes."

I cursed. "Even I'm not that fast."

Panther pulled away, tucking in his shirt and then running a hand over his close-cropped hair. He'd paired a blue collared shirt that matched his eyes with black slacks, looking every bit the sexy, put-together Navy pilot I knew him to be. Me, on the other hand? A new pair of jeans was as far as I wanted to go if I didn't have to put on my dress whites.

"Have I told you that you look sexy as fuck tonight?" I said.

"You might've mentioned it a few times."

"Just making sure you know so when Ace Locke undresses you with his eyes, you know I did it first."

Panther snorted, his head falling back as he laughed. "You're delusional."

"Yet the Navy lets me fly a fifty-two-million-dollar jet."

"Like I said: delusional." With a twinkle in his eye, Panther brought our joined hands up to his mouth and pressed a kiss to the back of mine. "Don't worry. I don't plan to leave you for anyone tonight."

"Mhmm. Just so you know, if you do run out on me, I'm taking your Christmas present back. And trust me, you want it."

"I thought this was my present?"

"It's the cherry on top."

"Gentlemen," the driver said over the intercom. "We've arrived."

I looked out the window to see the massive arena

looming overhead, red and green spotlights flashing across it and up into the sky. Ornamental balls that were probably bigger than the limo hung at intervals across the front, along with an oversized Christmas tree framing the entrance.

There were people everywhere, long lines out of at least half a dozen doors for those trying to get inside, while others wrapped around the hot chocolate and cider stands set up every few feet. Others milled around in their ugly Christmas sweaters, watching the already crowded ice rink that had been set up for the occasion.

Panther let out a low whistle. "L.A. doesn't know how to do things on a small scale, huh?"

"Those are the biggest fucking balls I've ever seen. Where the hell do people find shit like that?"

"Jealous?" Panther teased, as my door popped open. I downed the rest of my champagne and stepped out of the limo to see a gorgeous blond woman standing on the curb waiting for us. She wore a red long-sleeved reindeer-print dress that looked like one of the ugly Christmas sweaters I'd seen others wear, only it barely covered her ass and hugged her fit body tight. Paired with thigh-high boots, she looked like there should be a whip in her hand, not a clipboard.

"You must be Mateo and Grant," she said, giving us a brilliant smile as she stepped forward to shake our hands. "I'm Paige, and I'm here to show you fellas a good time."

When I raised my brows and heard Panther choke behind me, she laughed.

"And by that, I mean bypass the line and show you inside." She inclined her head for us to follow her through the crowd, dodging the already-buzzed guests holding their drinks precariously. Guess those hot chocolate stands had a vodka option.

Paige led us past the long lines to an unmarked door, flashed a badge across the scanner, and ushered us inside. The Christmas tunes that had been blaring outside followed us down a long hallway that opened up to the main floor of the arena, and once I got a good look inside...holy hell. It was something out of a Griswold fantasy. There were trees encased in fairy lights from top to bottom lining the perimeter of the arena, with clouds of snow gathered around the trunks. Icicle lights dripped off the tree branches, and even more hung down from the ceiling, like we were in a snow globe or some kind of winter wonderland.

"Wow," Panther said, and I had to agree. It was all you could do to just stare at the transformation of a place that usually hosted basketball games.

Paige beamed. "Thank you."

I did a double take. "You did this?"

"Well, I'm not just a pretty face," she said with a wink. "Now, the two of you will have your meet-and-greets later on this evening, but I think the plan is to get you all liquored up first and enjoying the party. And, if I may so say myself, it *is* a pretty fabulous shindig."

"I don't even know where to go first," Panther said, sounding utterly entranced. I laced my fingers through his and squeezed, and the smile that lit his face was worth every second of stalking the radio station.

"The concert starts soon, so if I were you, I'd go ahead and indulge." Paige pointed to a huge bar set up on one side of the room. "Licked is where you'll be able to grab a Locke

Licker or a Santa's Coming. Or a Grinch's Jingle Balls, if that suits your fancy."

My brow furrowed. "Are you talking about drinks?"

"Only the best drinks, courtesy of my best friend, Ryleigh. Tell her I sent you. And then over there we have catering by *the* Julien Thornton, one of the hottest chefs in the country. And I'm not just talking about his food," she said. "Feel free to mingle, check out the items up for auction, do a twirl around the ice rink, dance, strip down to your Santa boxers. Anything goes." Paige turned to leave. "Oh, and someone will grab you later to take you backstage, and you'll pick up your VIP bags there too."

"VIP bags?" I said.

"Of course. You don't think we'll let you boys leave empty-handed, now do you?" She laid a hand on Panther's arm. "Oh my." She squeezed his bicep and looked my way. "Aren't you a lucky pair. Mmm."

Dropping her hand, Paige smiled again, and I was glad I wouldn't have to peel her fingers off my man. Though she seemed more appreciative than interested in either of us, which I supposed was flattering. I mean, Panther *was* the hottest fucking man on the planet, so I couldn't exactly blame someone for noticing.

"You two have a fabulous time. I'm sure I'll run into you later." With a final wink, Paige headed off, and I squeezed Panther's fingers.

"I feel like I should've hired a bodyguard for tonight. No one's going to be able to keep their eyes or hands off you."

Grinning, Panther wrapped his arms around my waist and pulled me in close. I didn't think I'd ever get over how far we'd come, from having to hide our relationship while we competed against each other in the Elite program at NAFTA to being so open together in public. It wasn't something I'd ever take for granted.

"And here I thought you were my personal bodyguard," Panther murmured as he nipped at my lip.

"Oh, I'll happily guard this body, don't you worry about that." I reached down to grab Panther's ass and gave him a long, lingering kiss. Another thing I'd never get tired of: Panther's full lips.

He leaned back an inch and smiled. "You ready to get this thing started?"

"Hell yes. Where to first?"

As my stomach let out a loud rumble, he laughed. "I'm thinking we should check out this world-class chef and then maybe grab one of those Grinch drinks Paige was talking about."

"Perfect." I stole another quick kiss and then reached for his hand again. "Let's go see what this Julien guy's got in store for us."

THIRTEEN

"*H*OW LONG DID Jules say he'd be?" Robbie asked as we headed toward the front entrance of the large arena. Julien had left brunch early to check up on his staff, who were catering the charity event, and his absence was now being felt as Robbie and I headed toward our destination for the evening.

I tugged Robbie's hand up to my lips to kiss. "Not too long, a couple of hours, maybe? And he's already been gone—"

"One and a half." Robbie pouted, his slicked-up lips that matched his Santa hat beckoning me closer.

I leaned in to place my lips at the corner of his. "I miss him too."

It was true. The three of us were so tightly knit that when one of us wasn't around it felt like part of us was missing, especially when it came to events and holidays. But we'd catch up with our delicious chef soon enough. For now I needed to find something to distract Robbie with, since the actual concert didn't start for another hour or so.

People dressed in festive hats, tinsel scarfs, ugly Christmas sweaters, and signs with *I love Fallen Angel* walked toward the entryway along with us, all heading for the lines that led into the arena. Christmas music poured out of the speakers, and red and green lights lit the place up so bright that I was positive you'd be able to see it from outer space tonight.

I was about to guide Robbie to one of the lines so we could make our way inside, when he tugged on my hand and drew me to a stop.

"Everything okay, sweetheart?"

Robbie turned his pretty face toward mine and nodded. "Mhmm. I just worked out what we could do to pass some time."

I could think of several things we could do, but judging by the mischievous grin on Robbie's face, I had a feeling he was thinking of something completely different. "And what's that?"

He tugged on my hand until I looked to the left of the arena, where there was an...ice-skating rink. "No."

"I haven't even said anything yet."

"You don't have to. I know you, and the answer is no."

Robbie frowned and let go of my hand to cross his arms over his chest. "Um, excuse me, you don't get to just say no and that be the end of that."

My lips twitched at the sassy eyebrow winging up over his eye. I reached out to smooth my fingertip along it. "Yes, I do."

Robbie swatted at my hand and pointed at me. "No, you don't. You *owe* me."

"I owe you?" I chuckled. "And how do you figure that? Julien and I whisked you away for a surprise romantic weekend where you got to eat brunch with Ace Locke."

"That right *there*," Robbie said, finger pushing against my chest. "I had no warning, no chance to dress to impress. You two just sprang it on me, and I acted like a fool."

I took hold of his finger. "You always impress, dressed or not. And I didn't think you were foolish at all. I thought you were adorable."

"You have to say that; you're married to me." Robbie aimed a coy look at me from under his lashes. "And speaking of being married, haven't you heard the saying, happy wife, happy life?"

"Are you trying to tell me you aren't happy?"

"No, but I could be happier."

I sighed and looked over his shoulder toward the rink. "I don't ice-skate."

"You don't— You live in Chicago, where there is snow up to your waist half the year."

"Slight exaggeration, don't you think?"

"Okay, maybe a quarter of the year. You seriously don't ice-skate?"

"I wasn't born in Chicago, remember? Louisiana and California don't exactly have huge amounts of snow every year."

If I thought that was going to save me, I was gravely mistaken. The idea had already taken root with Robbie, and there was no swaying him.

"That's okay, I'll help you." He took hold of my hand and

began tugging me toward the outdoor rink, where people were skillfully gliding and weaving their way around the ice as though they'd been doing it their entire life.

There was no way in hell I was going out there.

"I have an idea. I'll stand over there by the rail and watch you," I said as we moved into line to pay for the skate rentals. "You know how much I like watching."

"Nice try, but no. You owe me, and this is what I want." Robbie squeezed my hand and gazed up at me with wide, hopeful eyes. "Come on, Joel. It's Christmas."

It was clear that he had my number and knew it. I didn't think there was anything I'd deny him when he looked at me that way. "Okay."

"Okay?" Robbie all but bounced on his toes. This was going to be awful—and probably painful—but I would have agreed a hundred times over to see him so happy.

I gestured to the counter, where it was our turn to order our shoes and pay, and ten minutes later they were on our feet and Robbie was urging me to stand.

I looked at the skates and grimaced. This was not going to be pretty.

"Come on," Robbie urged. "Don't be scared."

I aimed my most fulminating look his way, and when Robbie's lips twitched, I shook my head. "I don't think this is such a good idea."

"What do you mean? It's a fabulous idea."

Robbie held his hand out, and as I gingerly got to my feet, I swayed a little. Robbie's eyes widened and he moved forward to steady me. Shit. I wasn't even on the ice yet, for fuck's sake.

"Don't you dare laugh at me."

Robbie bit down on his lower lip, clearly trying to hold back a chuckle. "I would never."

"Liar," I muttered as he guided me toward the gate to hell. When he stepped out onto it and smoothly glided to the edge of the rink to wait for me, I tried to remember why I'd agreed to this again.

"Come on," Robbie said. "Just take it nice and slow. I'm right here."

I warily lifted a foot and slowly placed it on the icy ground, doing my best to block out the people twirling and jumping all around us. *Showoffs.*

"That's it. There's a nice break coming up. Just hold on to the edge and gently slide your— Whoa."

My feet scissored apart further than I would've liked, and Robbie lurched forward, placing a hand under my elbow.

"I got you," he said as his grip tightened and he guided me to the wall.

I took a death grip on the rail and tried to calm my pounding heart. *Jesus, please don't let me break anything.* Robbie slid in nice and close to me and ran his hand down my arm to entwine our fingers.

"Thank you for doing this with me."

I eyed him like he was out of his mind. "Don't thank me yet. This might be as far as I get."

"Maybe, but the fact that you're even standing here on wobbly legs gripping the rail like a lifeline means the world to me."

"Robert..."

He grinned like an imp, his rosy cheeks now cool from the ice. I leaned in to press a kiss to his lips.

"I'm going to pay you back for this," I promised.

"I sure hope so." He pulled back and then straightened. "Want to try moving from the rail?"

"Is that a trick question?"

Robbie held his hand out and gestured for me to come to him, and when I reached for his hand, he said, "Okay, now slowly slide your foot like this. Left then right. Got it?"

I did. But understanding and executing it were two completely different things. Praying someone with a gigantic blowtorch would come and melt this icy torture rink away, I did as I was told and hesitantly pushed off the rail.

My legs swayed in an unfamiliar way beneath me, and as I did my best to do what Robbie had suggested, my left leg shot out one way as my right went the other.

Robbie grabbed my elbows and pulled me to him, somehow managing to keep the both of us upright as I clung like a vine to his neck. This was completely and utterly humiliating, but when he rubbed his cheek up against my stubble and purred, I found one positive out of the moment. We were now standing as close as we could get with our clothes on.

"That was good," he said.

"That was almost a hospital visit."

"No." Robbie pulled back and ran his fingers down my cheek. "This is a moment. One I'll never forget. Thank you."

The genuine pleasure in his sparkling eyes made my discomfort totally worth it. We stood under the twinkle lights with "All I Want for Christmas Is You" playing on the speakers and people whizzing by us. "You're welcome."

Robbie gently let me go and grinned as he skated a little ways back from me. I frowned, and then he pulled his phone out and snapped several photos of me trying to stay upright, then skated around me, narrating a quick video to Julien.

When he was done, he slipped the phone into his pocket and skated back up to me.

"I take that back. You're not welcome at all."

He giggled and took my hand. "Hey, there's no way I wasn't going to get proof of this."

"Me skating?"

"No. How much you must love me."

That would be a whole hell of a lot, because there was no way I would've fallen on my ass *twice* in the ten minutes after that for just anyone—and Robert Thornton-Priestley knew it.

FOURTEEN

ACE

"OKAY, HOW DO I look?" I could hear the excitement of the audience beyond the curtain, the arena now filled with a festive crowd as the Jingle Ball was about to begin.

"Handsome as always." Dylan ran a hand down the sleeve of my red button-up shirt and squeezed my hand. "I still think you should wear the Christmas hat Paige offered. I am."

"Yes, but you look adorable. I, well… The blinking lights would've distracted me."

"Suuure. Keep trying with that excuse, but I know better. You work in front of lights and cameras for a living."

"Fine, so I didn't want to mess up my hair."

Dylan eyed my closely cropped hair and smirked. "More like you didn't want to look—"

"Ridiculous?"

"Aww, where's your Christmas cheer?"

80

I took hold of Dylan's chin and angled his face up toward mine. "I'm saving all my Christmas cheer for you...later."

Dylan's eyes sparked with mischief. "*And* your big candy cane?"

I chuckled. "Definitely. And if you don't mention the hat again, I might even let you suck it."

"Ace? Dylan?" Paige's voice made me look over my shoulder. "You ready?"

"Ready," we said at the same time, and then she frowned.

"Ace, where's your hat?"

"Umm..." I feigned ignorance and took a step back toward the stage. "Don't know, but—"

"Ace and Dylan, you're on," the stage manager said, just in the nick of time.

I gestured over my shoulder with my thumb. "I gotta go."

Her eyes narrowed, but before she could tear me a new one, I grabbed a grinning Dylan's hand and led him with me onto the stage.

The second we appeared, the excited crowd turned to a crazed one. The audience erupted with cheers, clapping, stomping feet, and catcalls. The spotlights followed the two of us to the center of the stage, and as we looked out at the winter wonderland Paige had created, I couldn't help but admire her skill. Damn, she was really good at her job. She'd turned a sporting arena into something out of everyone's Christmas fantasy.

"Good evening, everyone," I said into the mic, and when the cheering got louder, I chuckled. "Are we all feeling merry tonight?"

A unanimous *Yes!* boomed back at us as though it was

through a megaphone, and Dylan grinned and leaned into the mic.

"Sounds like it to me. And who wouldn't be feeling the Christmas spirit? Look at this place."

"I know." I took in the icicles hanging from the roof, the snowy trees flanking the arena's sides, and the blue and white wristbands flashing from the crowd. "I feel like I've stepped inside a snow globe. Let's give it up for the mastermind behind this whole event, Paige Dawson. She's really outdone herself."

The crowd agreed wholeheartedly. Dylan and I looked to the wings, where Paige gave a mock curtsy and then shooed us along. Of course she didn't want to stop and take in the praise—it would throw her carefully planned schedule all out of whack. We couldn't have that.

"Now that that's been said, welcome everyone to the Jingle Ball. We have some seriously exciting things happening tonight to raise money for many of the nonprofit organizations around the country that are struggling. From the hunger crisis, to the LGBT youth on the streets, and the arts that have taken a huge hit this year. Know that the money you paid to come and be with us tonight is going to a good cause, a worthy cause, a cause to help your fellow man. And we couldn't be more thrilled that you decided to come and spend your Saturday night with us."

"Ace couldn't be more right," Dylan said. "We are beyond thrilled. We are thankful and grateful to each and every one of you for choosing to come out tonight and give back to your community. After all, that's what Christmas is all about. Spreading the cheer and good fortune, and tonight we are going to do just that."

Clapping and cheering rang out as we stood there drinking in the joy filling the air, and I couldn't have been happier in that moment.

"Tonight there will be an auction with some fantastic prizes up for grabs."

"They really are fantastic," Dylan agreed. "You know that yummy food you've been eating all night? You have a chance to bid on an all-expenses paid dinner at JULIEN."

"Mmm, I might have to try for that one. The food at JULIEN is the best I've ever tasted. *Or* if you're looking for love and someone to maybe take *to* JULIEN, there's free matchmaking up for grabs."

Dylan grinned up at me as the crowd went nuts, and I chuckled.

"Yes, and there also happens to be a pair of VIP tickets for the next concert of a certain *band* that may or may not be here tonight—"

"*Fallen Angel! Fallen Angel!*" the crowd chanted.

I looked to Dylan. "Is that right?"

"It sure is. And not only will you get VIP tickets, you also get to meet them!"

The roar from the arena was so loud that it all but made the stage vibrate.

"Exciting, right? And there's a whole slew of other prizes in the mix also, but we'll tell you about them later, because as much as we love talking to you, I'm almost *positive* we are not the ones you want singing."

"He's right." Dylan winked at the crowd. "There's a reason he went into acting."

"I admit it, singing is *not* my strong suit. But I think we have a solution to that problem. Are you guys ready to get tonight started?"

Dylan and I laughed as the hooting and hollering echoed around the arena. As someone who played to a camera for a living, I was used to attention. But I couldn't imagine what it was like to play to an audience this big—and larger—on a nightly basis. The energy was palpable, the adrenaline easy to get caught up in, and when I leaned down and said into the mic, "Please help us welcome Fallen Angel," the thunderous response nearly blew us off the stage.

FIFTEEN

LOGAN

THE LIGHTS WENT low, a hush fell over the arena, and the crowd around us began to scream with excitement. Ace—*that bastard*—had given Tate a pair of VIP tickets before we'd left brunch, and that had us close enough to the stage that by the end of tonight I wouldn't be able to hear for a year.

That didn't seem to bother Tate in the least, however, as he wrapped his leather-clad arms around my waist and moved in behind me.

"You excited?"

I glanced back to see a wide smile on his sexy lips. "About standing so close to the stage that I'm likely to get sprayed with sweat?"

Tate chuckled and nuzzled against the collar of my black button-up shirt. "I've never known you to be worried about a little sweat. Plus, it's Fallen Angel. People would kill to be covered in their sweat."

"Not this person. I don't even know who they are."

"Yes, you do. I play them all the time at the bar. 'Invitation'? 'Hard'? I know you know that last one—you told me the lyrics were just your kind of filthy."

"Maybe, but that doesn't change the fact that there's only one person's sweat I'd kill to be covered in."

Tate pressed a hard kiss to my lips, and my cock throbbed in response. "How about you stand here and pretend to enjoy it while I grind all over you? I promise to get hot and sweaty with you after."

I groaned and slid my tongue inside his mouth for a deeper taste, and when he rubbed his erection up against the tailored black pants covering my ass, I pulled back. "Fine. But don't start something I'm gonna have to wait hours to be able to finish. It's just mean."

"Yeah, but that's half the fun."

I was about to turn around and show Tate the exact kind of *fun* I was interested in when a piano riff began to play over the speakers and the crowded arena erupted in a frenzy of cheers and wolf whistles.

A spotlight then lit up the center stage, and there, sitting behind a gleaming white piano with wings soaring high up into the sky, was a man with his head bent down over the keys. With blond curls falling down all around his face, and dressed in all white, the guy could've passed for a higher being as he continued to play a melody that sounded like the stuff of angels. Then the drums, keyboards, and guitars entered the mix and the blond looked up and began to sing.

Damn, okay, there was no mistaking how *this* band had gotten its name, because the man behind that piano looked and sounded like some kind of heaven-sent creature.

"Remember them now?" Tate said by my ear.

I shook my head, my eyes fixated on the blond stepping out from behind his piano and making his way up to the front of the stage.

"But if I knew blondie up there was in the band, I would've paid *much* more attention. Look at those curls."

Tate flattened his hands against my abdomen and pulled me back into him as the song continued. "How about you *stop* looking at those curls?"

"But you told me to enjoy it." And suddenly I was.

The members of the band had now moved to the front of the stage, and as the angel in white sauntered up to the surly guitar player standing directly in front of us, I couldn't take my eyes off them.

Mr. Surly had long, dark hair that fell down around his cheeks and chin, and the comparison of his devilish looks with the pure white angel rubbing all over him was hot as hell.

Tate's lips on my neck made me rock back into his body in time to the music as he slid his hand down to massage my throbbing cock. The angel's eyes locked on us, and then he gave a wicked smile and slid an arm around his guitar player's chest.

Mr. Surly tipped his head back against the angel's shoulder, and when the angel licked a path up his guitarist's neck, Tate squeezed his fingers around me.

Fucking hell. Tate hadn't told me this band was scorching hot. But suddenly I didn't care if I went deaf—my only hope was that I didn't go blind...

PANTHER

"OKAY, WE'RE SO close to the stage that I think we were just breathing the same air as Ace Locke." Solo grinned at me as the lights dimmed, and the excitement in the crowd hit an all-time high. "Fallen Angel is about to be right *there*."

It wasn't often that I got to see Solo as tripped up as he was now. As he bounced on the balls of his feet in an effort to make himself taller, I couldn't help but laugh. He was pumped, like he was about to strap himself into a fighter jet and blast up into the sky.

I took hold of his hand, not quite believing I was about to see Fallen Angel perform mere feet from me. But when "Invitation"'s piano intro boomed out through the arena, I squeezed my fingers around Solo's and strained to see whatever was about to happen on that mammoth stage.

Like a calling card to all Fallen Angel fans around the world, the familiar tune echoed around the sparkling arena then the stage lit up, and there he was—Halo.

The man dubbed "angel" by his boyfriend—and now the world—sat at his piano with his angel wings flanking him, and when Slade joined in with a thumping rhythm on his drums, the rest of the stage lit up and Solo and I shouted at the top of our lungs.

This was unfuckingreal. With the buzz of alcohol and the thrill of seeing one of our all-time favorite bands, the high coursing through me was out of this world.

A feast for the eyes and ears, it was hard to drink it all in as colored lights and massive screens on either side of the stage switched between videos and Halo as he made his way out from behind the piano and headed toward the front of the stage.

Killian and Viper commanded either side of the stage with a confidence that was enviable, and Jagger added a sexy sophistication that made this band not only talented but hot as hell.

Solo looked over at me and grabbed hold of my face to kiss me hard and fast. When he pulled away and laughed before turning back to the stage, I wrapped an arm around him and pulled him in front of me. I needed my hands on him, needed him to know just how much I was enjoying this moment here with him, because there was nowhere on earth I'd rather be.

We sang every single word at the top of our lungs along with the thousands of people here with us, and when Halo began to get all hot and heavy with his man on stage, the crowd went crazy.

It was a testament to how far we'd come that the most famous *gay* action star in Hollywood had just introduced the worldwide rock phenomenon Fallen Angel, who had several out and proud members. It was also one of the reasons I had such admiration for them.

These guys gave zero fucks, and when I thought back to the struggle Solo and I had faced when we first got together, it made me appreciate their openness even more.

"They're amazing!" Solo shouted. Halo moved to Killian and turned around so they were back to back, and then he belted out one of the highest notes I'd ever heard.

Amazing was an understatement. Fallen Angel had taken on legendary status in my mind, and even though they'd only been together for a short amount of time, I had no doubt that years down the track we'd all be watching them get inducted into the Rock and Roll Hall of Fame.

As the song slowed to the bridge, the crowd pulled their cell phones out and began to sway in time with Halo's voice. I wound my arms around Solo's waist and placed my lips to his temple and sang, "I want to be the one to make you fall from grace..."

Solo swayed in time with me and turned so our lips met. "I'm pretty sure that was the other way around."

I grinned against his mouth, thinking back to the first time I'd seen Solo's devil-may-care smile, and nodded. "Yeah, I think you might be right. Solo?"

"Hmm?"

"I love you."

"I love you too."

We smiled at one another, looked back to the stage, and watched as Halo sang the final lines of his love song to Viper, and again I was struck by the enormity of the moment.

Here we were surrounded by a crowd of people who didn't care one way or another who went home with whom. You could love who you wanted to love without fear or preju-dice, and that just made this night even more of a celebra-tion in my eyes.

JULIEN

"I THINK YOU and Paige have everything under control, Giselle. It looks wonderful in here." I took a final look at the food being prepared for intermission, and couldn't have been more pleased. Not that I'd expected anything less. Giselle was a fantastic manager, and JULIEN Los Angeles's success was a testament to her fastidiousness and professionalism.

"*Merci*," she said, throwing out the only French word she knew with a grin. "Now, why don't you head back out to the concert and find your men? As much as I love seeing you in person, I want you to relax and enjoy. This is supposed to be a mini vacation. We've got this."

I took off my apron and handed it over to her. "*Oui*, I believe you do."

"Of course we do. Now go, go. You don't want to miss the opening act."

With a final goodbye, I left the catering in her very capable hands and headed off to track down my men. The arena was close to full capacity now as I made my way past *Licked After Dark*—the boozy shake and alcohol stand I was definitely going to bring Robbie to during intermission.

As Ace and Dylan took the stage, I hurried over to the west entrance, where I caught sight of Robbie's Christmas hat and Priest's thick auburn hair. They were exactly where they'd said they'd be. Priest looked over and spotted me, and the smile on his usually stern lips made my heart thump.

In fact, the entire picture I was drinking in made my heart thump. Priest was standing behind Robbie with his arms wrapped around his waist, and Robbie was leaning back into him as he took a video of the crowd filling the decorated arena sprawling out in front of them.

I'd missed them the second I'd left them at Ace and Dylan's brunch, but there was something to be said for coming back together again.

"*Bonsoir*," I said as I stepped up by their sides, and Priest reached out to wrap an arm around my shoulders and pull me in close.

"*Bonsoir, mon coeur.* We missed you the last couple of hours, didn't we, sweetheart?"

Robbie turned so he was facing the two of us and nodded. "Terribly. It felt like days, not hours. No leaving, ever again."

I grinned and leaned in to kiss Robbie's rosy cheek. "That's what I like to hear from my men."

"It's true. So, is everything up to your standards?" Priest asked, as Robbie moved into the crook of my arm and hugged my side.

"It is. Giselle did a great job, and as you can see, Paige, who's running the event, is clearly at the top of her game."

"You're telling me. This place looks amazing. I've been taking videos to show everyone back home."

I squeezed Robbie's hand and then gestured toward the crowd. "I guess we should go find our spots."

Priest nodded and took Robbie's other hand, then weaved us through the crowd. When we reached the roped-off area of one of the VIP sections, we were ushered in just in time for Ace to exit the stage and the lights to go down.

Robbie squealed and jumped up and down, clearly thrilled with both his place in the crowd and what we were about to see, and a second later the heavenly notes of Fallen Angel's "Invitation" filled the arena.

I closed my eyes and let the melody wash over me, and when a loud gasp rippled through the crowd, I opened my eyes to see a piano on center stage that made my mouth fall open.

Mon Dieu. It was like something out of a dream. With feathered wings that looked ready to open up and carry the man at the piano off the stage, Halo looked ethereal, breathtaking, and one hundred percent the star he was.

The rest of the band joined him as soon as the drums kicked in, and as they really got into the heart of the song, they had the crowd eating out of the palms of their hands.

The song then shifted tempo and everyone pulled out their phones to sway along with Halo's angelic voice as he brought the song to a close.

"Good evening, L.A.!" he called out at the top of his lungs, and when everyone responded, he flashed a heart-stopping smile. "Thanks for coming out and spending your Saturday night with us! We know this is a Christmas concert and most of you are trying to be on your best behavior for Santa, but tonight I think we're gonna shake things up a little." He glanced over his shoulder to his bandmates. "What do you say, guys?"

"Hell yes," Viper responded. "Get them on that naughty list, Angel. That's where all the fun happens."

Halo turned back to face us. "So, what do you all say, L.A.? Want to get a little bit naughty with us tonight?"

The crowd boomed out a resounding *Yes!* and Robbie looked over his shoulder at Priest and I and waggled his brows. It was clear our *princesse* was ready and willing to do whatever it took to get on that list.

"Then what are you waiting for? We've got some balls to turn blue—*Christmas* balls. So guys, let's get 'Hard.'"

Viper's guitar growled through the stadium like a hungry beast as Slade started in with a pounding drum rhythm, accompanied by Killian's throbbing bass, and the only thought that came to mind with music like that was sex.

When Halo took the mic and started to sing about being sexually frustrated in the most indecent of ways, Robbie turned to Priest and me and made it his mission to put those words into action.

Rubbing his lithe body up against the both of us, Robbie did his best to drive the two of us out of our minds, and by the time the second chorus hit, we had him flush between us. Priest's eyes were steely grey, and his lips pulled tight as he moved along Robbie's back side and kissed his way up his neck. I, meanwhile, got the pleasure of feeling that lovely, hard cock of Robbie's rubbing against mine.

The flirt was incorrigible, and all I could think was thank God this was an eighteen-and-up charity event, because this song was set to make everyone in the room a little merrier— and hornier.

Robbie aimed a cheeky smile at me, his beautiful face full of arousal and pleasure, and just as I was about to indulge my desire to kiss his shiny lips, the music suddenly stopped and the spotlights, giant video screens, and icicles dripping from the ceiling above went out—and the arena plunged into darkness.

SIXTEEN

SHAW

"So AFTER THEY finish 'Get You Alone,' you'll come out for the duet," Paige said, showing the schedule on her clipboard to Trent. "Hopefully it'll run smoother than yesterday. After that, you're free."

Trent nodded as he shrugged on his leather jacket. "I talked to Kill earlier, and he assured me there wouldn't be an issue. We'll see about that."

"Please, God," Paige said under her breath before giving us a bright smile. "You guys all set? There's drinks and catering in the room next door, and if you need me, just let the stage manager know."

"Thank you, Paige. I'm sure you've got a million other things to take care of." I nodded in Trent's direction. "I can take it from here."

"Oh, I'm sure you can." She hugged the clipboard to her chest and looked me up and down. "It's gotta be helpful to have a boyfriend who's big enough to scare everyone off."

Trent laughed and caught my eye in the mirror as he straightened his cuffs. "It's a perk."

"You two sayin' I look scary?" I feigned offense.

"Nooo." Paige shook her head. "It's more the height and all those muscles. No offense to Trent, but I'm sure you could bench-press him for fun."

"You'd be right about that," Trent said, sidling up behind me and wrapping his arms around my waist. "It is fun."

With a laugh, Paige headed toward the door. "And on that note, I'm gonna leave you two to—"

Before she could finish, the room went dark and the sound of Fallen Angel playing onstage went dead silent.

"Oh shit." I could hear her fumbling with the door, and when she got it open and there was no light anywhere, she cursed again. Faint voices could be heard through her headset, and then, "The entire arena is dark?"

Fuckin' hell. I reached into my pocket for my cell phone and hit the flashlight so it illuminated the space, and the alarm I saw on Paige's face wasn't something I would wish on anyone.

The sound of the crowd beginning to panic filtered down the hall backstage, people obviously starting to freak out in the dark, which wasn't going to help anything at all.

"How soon do the backup generators go on?" Paige flipped on her own cell phone light and darted into the hallway toward the stage, as Trent and I followed behind her. "Five minutes? In five minutes, people will get trampled trying to leave—"

"Wait." Trent reached for her arm. "I have an idea." When he looked over his shoulder at me, I knew exactly what he was thinking and took off toward the crew backstage. They had what I needed—thank God—and when I ran back to Trent, I held up the battery-run floodlight.

"Babe, perfect," he said, and gave me a quick kiss. "Light me up and I'll take care of the rest. Paige—you good?" When she nodded, he shot me a wink. "Then let's do this."

With my cell phone light leading the way, he walked onto the stage, past the guys of Fallen Angel still standing in their places, waiting for the generators to kick in, but the crowd wasn't in the mood to wait, judging by the restlessness in the room. I dropped to the ground at the front of the stage in front of Trent and angled the spotlight toward him before flipping it on.

The moment Trent was lit up like a beacon in the darkness, the crowd began to hush, but then roared once they realized who it was surprising them on stage. It wasn't until Trent lifted his hand that the room once again quieted down, waiting to see what he'd do. Even without a microphone, the power of his voice could reach out across the arena, and he chose a song that would use that power to its fullest extent.

He'd barely gotten out the words "empty spaces" when cheers erupted from those closest to the stage. Trent had made the perfect choice: a Queen anthem the audience could sing along to.

As he reached the chorus of "The Show Must Go On," I chanced a look behind me to see that the arena was lighting up in a wave of cell phone lights swaying back and forth. The pride I felt in that moment wasn't unusual when it came to how I felt about Trent, but feeling the energy in the room turn from anxiety to excitement was overwhelming.

My guy was a real fucking rock star, and it had never been

more apparent than it was right then, with the entire arena singing along to his a cappella.

As the song continued, the power slowly began to come back on. In such a large space, it would take a few minutes for the twinkling lights to shine brightly again, so I kept the spotlight on Trent as Halo moved his microphone stand in front of him. His voice rang out clearly now, echoing out of the speakers into the arena, and seconds later, Killian joined in on his bass, followed by Slade on the drums. One by one, the rest of Fallen Angel joined in, even, to my surprise, Viper on guitar.

It felt like every person in the crowd was singing along, and as the icicle lights grew strong enough to see Trent, I turned off the floodlight and got to my feet. Before I could hightail it off the stage, though, Trent grabbed my hand and pulled me right back. He squeezed my fingers and grinned as he continued to sing, content for me to stand right there beside him in front of—

Jesus. I squinted as the massive crowd came into focus, and my knees suddenly felt weak. There were just so many people... How did Trent get up here and do this and *like* it?

I squeezed the ever-loving shit out of his hand, determined not to pass out and embarrass him during his big moment. Like he knew I was sweating bullets, Trent turned us so we were facing each other and finished off the song looking directly into my eyes. When he looked at me that way, nothing else existed. Not the others on stage with us, not the people watching. It was me and my guy, and he was serenading me like he'd done when I met him.

The deafening cheers once the song ended broke my trance, and Trent turned back to the crowd, waving and grinning like he knew he'd just saved the night. I couldn't even imagine the chaos if he hadn't thought fast and jumped on stage when he did.

"Thank you," he said, sending off another round of screams and applause that didn't die down as Paige walked toward us, a mic in hand.

"How about Trent fucking Knox?" she yelled, and this time I was sure I was going to go deaf. I'd be hearing these shouts echoing in my ears for days to come, but it was worth it to see my man get his due.

Yeah, proud was the understatement of a century.

SEVENTEEN

SWEET JESUS ON a crispy cracker, just when I thought it had all gone to hell in a handbasket, Trent Knox had gone and saved the day.

Yeah, he was definitely going on my Christmas card list.

"Okay, everyone, so that blackout was fun and all, but let's not do it again, yeah?" I said, and whoops rang out in response. "We've got so much more to come from these guys, but for now we're gonna let them go recoup while you get your refill on. Go visit my girl Ryleigh at the bar and get her to make you something naughty."

As Trent, Shaw, and Fallen Angel left the stage, I saw Ace and Dylan getting mic'd up in the wings. Okay, good, things were still somewhat on track, blackout be damned.

"In a few minutes, Ace Locke and Dylan Prescott will start the auction, so get ready to bid, and remember—this is all going to several of Ace's favorite charities, so don't get cheap on him."

Laughter met my ears as I headed backstage and

Christmas music once again filtered throughout the arena. For the moment I felt like I could breathe again after the heart attack the blackout caused, but I wouldn't let myself get overly cocky again for the rest of the night. Not until it all went off without another hitch and I could drink myself into oblivion after.

"That went well." Ace gave me a knowing grin as a crew member adjusted the mic on his collar. "Need a sedative yet?"

"Hopped up on adrenaline at the moment, but let me tell you—the crash later is going to be epic."

Dylan clucked his tongue. "Poor Dawson. Maybe he's the one who'll need the sedative."

"Nah. Ryleigh's kept him occupied at the bar all day, and by occupied, I mean heavily intoxicated. Lucky bastard." I let out an exaggerated sigh and clapped my hands together. "So, you two ready to raise some serious money?"

"Yup," Ace said, waving the auction list he held. "And if all else fails and the bids aren't high enough, Dylan will do a striptease."

Dylan's jaw dropped. "I'll do what?"

"Nothing says merry Christmas like a naked man." I nodded. "Do what you need to."

"Listen, Hotshot, if you think me getting naked would raise more than you taking off your pants, you've got another thing coming."

Ace laughed at Dylan's protests as the sound guys finished their job.

"You want an intro?" I asked, and Ace shook his head.

"Nah, we've got this." He took hold of Dylan's hand, linking their fingers. "Don't we, Daydream?"

As they headed toward the stage, I could hear Dylan say, "Seriously, if anyone is getting naked tonight, it's you."

Ahh. Decisions, decisions.

I hit the mic button on my headset. "Auction in five... four...three...two..."

Screams filled the air as Ace and Dylan hit the stage, and, no longer needed backstage, I quickly made my way through the back hall to join everyone on the floor of the arena. I needed to make sure the auction went smoothly, and thank God my team knew that, because anytime someone had a question or needed assistance, one of my managers went running.

By the time I hit the floor, the guys were already in full swing on the first item, a signed guitar from our blackout savior Trent Knox.

As the bids surpassed two thousand dollars, Ace held his finger up to his ear like he was getting an incoming message.

"What's that? Trent will personally deliver the guitar to you after the show? And it'll be the one he's using tonight?"

Instantly, the shouts started up again, each person yelling out a bid also holding up an auction paddle with their special number on it. Wait, why the hell hadn't I thought to get myself a damn paddle?

After an aggressive bidding match, Dylan pointed to a woman near the front of the stage. "Sold to number five forty-eight. Trent Knox's guitar and all his sweat from tonight is yours. Stand by and one of our volunteers will be by to get your information."

Not bad. These guys were better at this than I thought.

"Next up," Ace said, looking down at the list. "An all-expense-paid private dinner for you and an unlimited number of guests at one of Julien Thornton's signature restaurants around the country." He raised his brows at Dylan. "I think we might have to take this one."

"Oh hell no," came a shout from the audience, and I would've recognized that voice anywhere. Logan Mitchell had a drink in one hand and his paddle raised in the other. "Ten thousand dollars."

Dylan let out a low whistle. "All right, then. The bidding begins at ten grand."

"Twelve," Logan yelled again, and this time, Ace laughed and looked down at his friend.

"Bidding against yourself tonight, Mitchell? Wanna make it thirteen?"

"Thirteen," someone else shouted, and Logan slowly looked over his shoulder.

"Thirteen five," came another bid, and that person also got the Logan Mitchell death glare.

Yeah, I didn't want to be on the receiving end of that look.

Logan's paddle went up in the air again and he shouted, "Fourteen thous—"

But he wasn't able to even get the words out before he was being outbid again.

Aaand that was the wrong thing to do, because Logan yelled, "Fifteen fucking thousand," while staring down the others who had been trying to horn in on what he perceived as his prize. Seconds went by as everyone seemed to collectively hold their breath, waiting to see if anyone would dare top that, and when no one held up a paddle, Ace said, "Sold for fifteen thousand dollars to the madman in the glasses."

As Logan lifted his glass and smirked triumphantly, Tate

looked at his husband with a mixture of admiration and amusement. I could only imagine he leaned in to whisper in his ear that he was fucking crazy, because that was exactly what I'd be saying. But hey, it was for charity, so good on him.

Everything after that ran smoothly, more money being raised than even I'd expected, but just as the last item went up for grabs, all hell broke loose.

"Now for this final item," Dylan said, "Ace has offered the highest bidder a walk-on role for one of his upcoming films. That means you could brag to all of your friends and family that you starred in a movie with Ace Locke." Dylan waggled his brows at Ace. "I'm sure he'd even throw in one of his delicious bear hugs while you're on set too. Let the bidding begin."

Our VIP guests, Solo and Panther, threw up their paddles immediately, as well as about a hundred others, but it was Slade from Fallen Angel running out to the stage that caught everyone's attention.

"It's mine." Slade was panting, like he'd had to haul ass running to catch the auction in time, and he gave an apologetic look to the audience. "Sorry, but this is too good to pass up."

"You can't win without a bid, Slade," Dylan said.

"Oh, right." Slade rubbed his jaw, his brow furrowed. "I guess twenty?"

"Twenty thousand?"

"Yeah. Is that enough?"

Before Dylan could confirm it, a bid of twenty-two came from someone in the audience, and thus began another bidding war, Slade going head to head with the others vying for a chance to be in an Ace Locke picture.

Just when it looked like Slade was going to win this round, the number already growing to obscene levels, another player entered the game.

"Fifty thousand." Jagger stepped out from backstage, giving Slade a shit-eating grin.

Slade's eyes widened. "You asshole. I told you this one was mine."

"Well, I decided I wanted it too. Besides, my face would look better onscreen."

The audience roared as the two Fallen Angel members went at it, throwing jabs at each other and upping the bid to levels no one in the audience dared match.

Slade crossed his arms, looking intimidating as hell with his sky-high mohawk. "One hundred."

Jagger, unfazed, mimicked his pose across the stage. "One hundred one."

"One hundred two."

"One hundred ten."

"One hundred fifteen."

When Jagger opened his mouth to respond, Slade held up his hand. "Give it up, man. I'm not letting you win this."

"You don't have to *let* me win anything. I'll do it myself. One twenty."

Slade growled. "One twenty-five."

It was like we were all watching a tennis match, heads jerking back and forth, and it was so engrossing that none of us noticed when Killian walked out to stand beside Ace and Dylan.

"One fifty," he said, and as Slade and Jagger whipped their

heads around, their jaws dropped, so surprised that they couldn't get out a word as Dylan said, "Going once, twice, sold to Killian for one hundred and fifty thousand dollars."

If I'd thought Jagger had given a good shit-eating grin, it was nothing on the victorious smile Killian gave his fellow band members. It didn't last long, though, because Slade and Jagger both lunged in his direction, and Killian hightailed it off the stage before they could get their hands on him.

Part of me wondered if I needed to go back there and make sure they didn't kill each other, but one of my staff came over the headset and assured me she was backstage getting them ready to go back on.

Something told me she wasn't telling me the truth, because I'd seen the way they desperately wanted that prize, but this was a moment I was more than happy to delegate to others.

Ace was wrapping things up, and I was sure Dylan was grateful that he hadn't had to strip down to his skivvies after all. Damn shame for the rest of us, but c'est la vie.

"Thank you for being so generous tonight. You all still having a good time?" When the audience cheered their approval, Ace gave them a megawatt smile. "It's only going to get better, because hitting the stage again now—if they're not beating each other senseless after that bidding war—is Fallen Angel, with special guest Trent Knox!"

EIGHTEEN

DYLAN

"I'VE BEEN WAITING for this part of the show all night," I whispered as Ace and I moved behind the curtain to the left of the stage.

"I know. We're lucky it's even happening after that little power mishap."

"Little?" I slipped my arm through the crook of Ace's elbow and cuddled into his side. "We almost blew out L.A.'s entire power grid."

Ace chuckled. "Paige really outdid herself."

"Right? I still can't believe there wasn't a mass exodus."

"Agreed. Thank God for Trent. That could've been ugly."

"Speaking of Trent..." I gestured to where he was walking onto the dark stage to take up his place next to his old band's new frontman, Halo. It had to be weird, coming back to the group as an outsider, especially after all of the rumors that had swirled around his departure. But, selfishly, I couldn't wait to see him up there with Halo. The two of them together were going to be unreal.

Blue and white snowflake spotlights began to twinkle around the crowded arena as Jagger began the familiar keyboard intro to one of my all-time favorite Christmas songs, "Last Christmas." Then Trent stepped up to the mic and began to croon into it as *real* snowflakes began to flutter from the ceiling.

The smile on my face was so wide that I was positive it might slide right off it. The crowd erupted in cheers and applause and started to sing along with Trent. The classic rendition had always been my favorite, and I couldn't have been happier they'd decided to honor it.

Halo stepped forward to sing the first verse, reminiscing over being once bitten and twice shy, and holy wow, talk about a reception. It was clear the audience was as excited about seeing them both on that stage as I was.

Back and forth they switched off, their voices unbelievably in sync. They played off one another in the best ways imaginable, and when Halo made his way over to Viper to tell him that this year he was going to give his heart to someone special—and then added a kiss just so everyone knew who that *special someone* was—the crowd went wild.

"They're really incredible," Ace said by my ear, and I turned to look up at him and nodded.

"They really are. I can't believe how great they sound together. Hey, maybe they'll get Trent to go on tour with them sometime?"

Ace smirked and looked back to the stage. "I wouldn't hold your breath, Daydream. Just because Halo and Trent are getting along doesn't mean the rest of Fallen Angel is ready to welcome him back with open arms. Check out Viper."

I zeroed in on the devilishly good-looking guitarist, who

was watching Trent with narrowed eyes. Yeah, okay, there was no love lost there, but it was nice to imagine—if you didn't include the bloodshed that might follow.

When the song came to a close, the applause that echoed around the arena was almost deafening. Halo waved at them all as both he and Trent gave each other a mock bow—to which, I noted, Viper rolled his eyes.

Both men then turned back to their mics as a cozy fireplace appeared on each of the big screens flanking the stage. As the crackling of the wood sounded throughout the hushed arena, the scent of chestnut and pine seemed to fill the air, and I stood there in awe.

How the hell Paige had managed half of the things she had tonight was beyond me. But I was so thankful to be here enjoying the experience—it was one I knew I'd never forget as Halo and Trent began to sing the classic "Christmas Song."

I turned in Ace's arms and smiled at his handsome face. "Dance with me?"

He drew me into his strong arms and wrapped them around me, as I clasped my hands behind his neck and hummed along with the tune.

"This is nice."

Ace lowered his forehead to mine and closed his eyes. "It's perfect..."

Yes, it was. But then again, there was rarely a moment that wasn't perfect with my husband. Every day was better than the day before, and I knew this was just one more that we'd never forget.

Ace moved his lips to my ear and sang along with the two on the stage.

I grinned and pulled back. "Merry Christmas."

Ace lowered his mouth to mine, and as I melted in his embrace, we swayed with one another to the rest of the song. I couldn't help but feel disappointed as it came to an end.

I was about to tell Ace as much when the unmistakable sound of Viper playing the bluesy opening to "Run Rudolph Run" ripped through the air. Then Slade cut in on the drums and Killian and Jagger dove in headfirst.

Talk about waking the crowd up. In seconds, people were singing and dancing in the audience like they'd all been given a shot of adrenaline. Trent opened the song, keeping perfect pitch and time with the fast beat, and as he approached the chorus, he made his way over to Viper, who was going to town on the guitar.

The two had a kind of standoff before Viper turned his back and leaned into his ex-frontman, then he threw himself headlong into a guitar solo. It was hard to believe a Christmas song could be so kickass, but when Halo took up the second section, added this growly thing to his voice, and leaned into his mic as though it were just another appendage, I was floored.

Talk about stage presence. All six of these guys had it, and by the end of the song the crowd was beside themselves screaming out different songs they wanted to hear. Halo and Trent laughed at each other and feigned fatigue, Trent with a hand on his hip, Halo using his mic as support, then they grinned at each other and signaled Viper, who hit the guitar intro again at supersonic speed as the guys finished the night out with a final rapid-fire run through the chorus.

I hooted and hollered from our place in the wings, and Ace threw in a couple of wolf whistles as the guys waved to the crowd and thanked them all. They all began to make their way off the stage toward Ace and me, but at the last second, Viper stopped behind the mic Halo had vacated and looked out into the crowd.

"So, have you all had a good night tonight?"

When the crowd responded with a resounding *Yes!* he chuckled into the mic and nodded.

"I thought so. Me too. A night I'm not gonna forget anytime soon."

As the crowd nodded, Viper looked over to where the band was now watching him with confusion, and a smile curved his lips as he continued on.

"Which is why I'm not quite done with it yet. But for the final Christmas act, I think I'm gonna need an angel."

The response to that was immediate. Viper pointed to Halo and crooked his finger. Slade, who was standing in front of me and Ace, leaned into Jagger and whispered, "What the hell is going on?"

It seemed the only person who knew the answer to that was Viper, judging by Halo's expression. But I guessed we'd soon find out, because his angel was now moving out to take center stage.

NINETEEN

HERE GOES NOTHIN'.

"For my final Christmas act, I'm gonna need an angel." I crooked my finger, motioning for Halo to come join me center stage, and even though I knew I was throwing off nothing but confidence, a bead of sweat trailed down my neck at what I was about to do.

To say I'd been a ball of fuckin' nerves for days now might've been an understatement, but at least I'd had Trent around to blame for my mood. It had thrown everyone off the scent, especially Halo, which was why he was looking at me now with a crinkled brow and confusion in his eyes.

Oh, if he only knew. Which he would, in a matter of seconds.

Fuck if that didn't make my palms sweat to the point of needing to wipe them on my jeans.

Why the hell had I decided right here and now was the best time to pull this off? Oh, right. Not only was Christmas Halo's favorite holiday, but a big declaration like this told everyone who stared at him all dreamy-eyed to back the fuck off.

Taken. Mine. All those possessive terms I thought were bullshit before I met Halo were all I could think and feel anymore. I'd waited long enough to make things official between us. I wasn't wasting any more time.

"Goddamn, he's gorgeous, isn't he?" I shook my head as I stared at my guy, who turned ten shades of red as the crowd answered with wolf whistles and applause. I loved that even though his confidence onstage had grown in leaps and bounds since his time with Fallen Angel, he still got embarrassed when attention was focused directly on him for any reason other than singing. It was endearing and cute as hell —the complete opposite to me, but hey, that was why we worked, right?

I lifted the strap of my guitar over my head and handed it off to one of the stagehands, then did a quick swipe of my palms against my jeans. As I reached for Halo's hands, the hoots in the audience grew louder, like they could anticipate what was about to happen. Or maybe it was that they could hear how hard my heart was battering my chest through the microphone in front of me.

The last thing I'd expected was to be standing up here nervous as fuck. I'd thought about this moment for so long, but as the day drew closer, unfamiliar butterflies had begun to swarm in my stomach, and they were raging now.

He'll say yes, right? God, the thought of him turning me down hadn't even entered my consciousness before, and no way was I going to consider that option now.

I blew out a breath, getting myself back under control and focused on the man in front of me. From the first time

I'd seen Halo, all sweet innocence and golden curls, I'd been lost to him. At the time, I'd assumed whatever happened between us would be a casual thing, but then I'd caught feelings, and nothing had been the same since.

"Halo," I said, grinning like a fool already. I rubbed my thumbs along the top of his hands, and he swallowed hard, like he knew something big was coming. He didn't look out at whoever was watching us, only stared at me, waiting patiently.

"Hands down, you are the best fucking thing that's ever happened to me. I knew I was in trouble when I met you—I just didn't realize how much my life would change."

A shy smile lit up Halo's face, and he squeezed my fingers.

"I know I'm a selfish bastard, and I don't plan to stop being that way, because I want you with me every day, every night, every second. I want everyone to know you're mine, and I want a ring on your finger that you flash every time someone so much as looks your way."

Halo's eyes went wide as gasps rang out around the arena, and just like that, the secret was out.

I dropped down to one knee, only letting go of one of his hands so I could reach for the ring in my pocket. Halo's mouth parted as he got a good look at the platinum band gleaming under the stage lights, and then his eyes met mine.

"Yes," he whispered, nodding, and dammit, I couldn't stop my huge smile.

"Angel, I have to ask you first."

"Oh, right. Yes in advance, then."

Even though I'd blocked everyone else out, I could hear

the laughter and cheers at Halo's exuberance, and all those butterflies left my stomach permanently.

I brushed a kiss along Halo's knuckles and looked up at him. He even looked like an angel standing there staring down at me, the lights above him shining down to give him a halo around those curls. I'd never seen a more beautiful sight. He was perfect, and more than that, he was mine for the rest of our lives.

If I could manage to get the words out.

"Angel," I said, as a calm washed over me, and for the first time tonight, my voice was sure and steady. "It's no secret I want you to be mine forever. You make me a better man, which I know the rest of the guys are grateful for." I cracked a smile as Halo beamed. "But more than wanting you, I need you. Say you'll put me out of my misery and marry me."

I'd never seen a bigger smile on Halo's face as he nodded again and said, "Of course I'll marry you."

I was on my feet in half a second as the arena exploded into thunderous applause and cheers, and as I wrapped my arms around Halo, he grabbed my face and kissed the breath out of me. I didn't know how long we stayed tangled together, but when we finally broke apart, my head was spinning, my feet no longer touching the ground, or at least it felt that way.

Halo reached for my hand, the one still holding his ring. "You have to put that on me, you know."

Hell yes I did. I slid the band onto his left ring finger and kissed it for good measure before turning to the crowd.

"Officially off the market," I said, wrapping my arm around Halo's waist and pulling him tight to me. It was wild to see the look on everyone's faces: a mixture of shock, excitement, and, for some, crushing disappointment, I was sure.

Too. Damn. Bad.

Halo waved at the crowd as the rest of the band came running out on stage toward us, and right on cue, the curtain closed, blocking us all from view.

"Holy shit, why didn't you tell us?" Slade said. "Or did you all know?"

"I didn't know," Jagger said.

When Killian only smiled and didn't say anything, Slade glared his way.

"You knew?"

Killian rolled his eyes. "You think Viper could pick out a ring by himself? Come on."

"Speaking of rings," Jagger, ever the jewelry connoisseur, said. "Give us a look at the goods."

Halo held his hand out, proudly showing off the band that, yes, Killian had helped me pick out. In my defense, I knew it was the one when I saw it. I just wanted a second opinion.

Jagger whistled. "Now *that's* a nice ring, Viper. You did good."

"Only the best for my angel." I hugged Halo in even closer, not letting him go for a second.

"Viper engaged. Who would've ever thought it?" A new voice entered our circle, and I looked up to see Trent and his Herculean-sized boyfriend Shaw giving us amused smiles.

With a snort, I shook my head. "Not me."

"Well, congrats, man. I'm happy for you." Trent held his hand out toward me, and with the pressure off, I guessed I didn't mind the guy so much at the moment. I shook his hand, expecting that to be it, but then he surprised the shit out of me by pulling me in for a hug. Well, as much as he could with me still being attached to Halo.

As Trent clapped me on the back, he said, "I guess I kind of get you being an ass now."

"Me? An ass?" I pulled away from him and smirked. "Now that would be out of character."

"I just feel bad for Halo, being stuck with you."

"Happily stuck, you mean." My guy—*fiancé*—leaned in and kissed my neck, and I suddenly wished we were anywhere other than surrounded by a shit-ton of people.

"All right, are we done here? Nothing else we need to do, right?" I looked to Killian, who I knew would be on top of our schedule.

He shook his head. "Just a quick photo op with some winners and then you two can head out."

"Thank fuck." Those words out of Halo's mouth instead of mine made everyone bust a gut, and as we followed the others backstage to wherever the photo op was going to take place, I held tight to my present and future.

"I can't believe you did that," Halo said, holding on to me just as tight.

"Surprised?"

"Uh, yeah. No wonder you were acting crazy this week."

"More than usual?"

He laughed. "Oh yeah. But don't worry. You're forgiven."

With the others filing into a hallway up ahead, Halo moved us to a dark corner out of sight and pushed me up against the wall.

"I hope you know what you've gotten yourself into," he murmured before taking my lips with his. I sank into him, the way I always did when we got our hands on each other. Sensual and eager, ready to get out of here and go somewhere alone. "No getting rid of me now."

If he thought that was a warning, he'd lost his mind. "So you'll really marry me?"

Halo moved back enough that even in the darkness I could make out the twinkle in his eyes, and it was a look I knew I'd never forget.

"Yes," he said, bringing his lips back to mine ever so lightly. "A thousand times yes, Viper. I'm yours."

TWENTY

SOLO

TONIGHT HAD BEEN awesome. *Beyond* awesome. It had been fan-freaking-tastic. Meeting Ace Locke just now had been the cherry on top of the best sundae ever, and if the goofy grin on Panther's usually serious face was anything to go by, he was feeling the exact same way.

"Can you believe how nice he was?" I said as we stepped out of the lounge we'd just had our meet-and-greet in. Just like the rest of the place, it had been decorated like something out of a Hallmark Christmas movie. But unlike one of those flicks, the star of *our* show had been an A-grade Hollywood superstar.

"I know. He was so easy to talk to, it felt like we'd known him for years."

"Dylan too. That story about the Horny Goat weed was hilarious. Maybe we should look it up."

I scoffed. "You trying to say I don't have enough stamina?"

"Hell no. Any more energy from you and I'd never been able to leave the bed. I just think it'd be funny to check out."

I took Panther's hands in mine and pulled him to me. "Did you have fun tonight?"

His mouth kicked up at the sides, and when he lowered his head to brush his lips over mine, my cock throbbed. "More fun than I ever imagined possible. Thank you again. This Christmas is going to be pretty tough to beat next year."

I wound my arms around his neck and parted my lips for him to taste, and when his tongue slipped inside, I groaned. "You know me, always up for a challenge."

"Hmm, more like always *up*." Panther thrust his hips against mine, and what do you know, I wasn't the only flyboy here who was enjoying the moment.

"I can't deny it. You put your hands, mouth, or body anywhere close to mine, and what can I say, the response is automatic."

One of the hands under discussion moved down to my ass and pulled me even closer. "Something I will never complain about. So how about I take you back to the hotel and thank you properly?"

"Properly but not...proper, right?"

Panther kissed his way up my jaw to my ear and whispered, "I promise, nothing I plan to do to you when I get you in our room will be proper."

I was about to tell him that was more than okay with me when I heard—

"Grant? Mateo? Oh, thank God, I thought I missed you guys."

We pulled apart to see Paige running our way, and I was

impressed that anyone could run around the way she did in those thigh-high boots—the heels were insane.

"Sooo, how was it, how was it? Was Ace on his best behavior? Or perhaps his worst? Whatever floats your boat," she said, then added a sassy wink.

Panther moved to stand beside me and smiled. "He was fantastic. He's so easygoing."

"He really is, isn't he? Unless you side-eye or badmouth his Daydream, that is. Then he'll go total Hulk on your ass." She paused, seemed to think over her words, and then added, "Well, not your actual ass—but you get the point."

"We do, and seriously, this has been the best prize—and night—either of us have ever had."

A bright smile lit her beautiful face. "Now that makes me happy, and the fact that I can be happy after almost short-circuiting half of L.A. is saying something."

"Hey, you won't hear us complaining. We got to hear Trent Knox sing a Queen song. That was some kickass bonus material right there."

Paige nodded and let out a sigh. "You're right about that. He sure did save the night. Well, your limo is waiting for you where it dropped you earlier, and if you have any other questions about tonight—or want to write a glowing review on how awesome I was—you can find my website here on my card."

She took a business card from her clipboard and handed it to Panther.

"It was a pleasure meeting you two. If you'll excuse me, I'm going to go and down every leftover drink at the bar before crawling into bed and passing out for two weeks straight."

"Thanks again, Paige. We'll never forget this." I watched as she turned and headed back inside the venue, then I took Panther's hand in mine and grinned. "Ready to head out?"

"You bet. I have someone to thank over and over again."

TATE

"GO ON, YOU can say it..."

"I'm sorry." Logan gestured to his ear as the crowd began to disperse. "Can you speak up a little? I think I might be deaf."

I took his hand as we moved with the rest of the people leaving the VIP area. "You had a good time. Admit it."

Logan glanced at me out of the corner of his eye and shrugged. "I mean, it wasn't bad."

"Bullshit. You had a great time. I wish it was more because you were there with me than checking out the blond on stage, but..."

"You know better than that."

"Do I?" I did, of course. Logan wouldn't look twice at another man. Hell, he'd even spent fifteen thousand dollars to rent out JULIEN back in Chicago for a private dinner with me. But it was too much fun playing with him this way. "You *were* looking at him pretty hard."

"He was the lead singer."

"Of a *band*. Or did you miss the other people on stage with him?"

Logan looked at me as though I'd lost my mind.

"Are you really trying to tell me you're upset I was watching the band?"

"Watching them? No. But I thought you might cry when Viper proposed to Halo."

When Logan realized I was kidding, his eyes narrowed on me.

"If it'll make you feel better, I could dye my hair blond when we get back to Chicago."

"Don't you fucking dare."

"No?"

"Not if you want to sleep in my bed at night."

I slipped an arm around his waist. "Oh, I definitely want to be there at night. During the day, too."

Logan groaned and grabbed the edges of my leather jacket. "Good answer."

"Yeah?"

"Yeah."

"And you really don't want the young blond over me?"

Logan's smile was downright wicked. "The only thing I want over you is me. So let's get the hell out of here."

"Logan! Tate!"

We turned to see Robbie, Julien, and Priest making their way toward us. They'd been in a different section than the two of us tonight, but as we got outside the main doors, we waited for them to exit with the rest of the crowd.

When they finally reached us, Julien smiled and looked between the two of us. "*Bonsoir*. Did you two enjoy the show?"

I smirked and side-eyed my husband, who said, "Parts of it."

"*Parts* of it?" Robbie frowned. "It was unreal."

"Yeah, well, a certain blond with curls made tonight particularly enjoyable for Logan."

"Ah. Got a crush on Halo, huh?"

"He did...until he got engaged."

Priest chuckled as he pulled Robbie in under his arm. "Well, don't let that stop you. Maybe you could become a foursome? Just think, Tate, another couple of people would help take him off your hands occasionally."

Logan glared at his work partner and friend. "Tate likes his hands just fine on me, thank you very much. I was just admiring the lead singer. He was very...talented."

That made me laugh, because the last thing that had captured Logan's attention was the music Halo had been playing. But deciding to give him a break, I switched subjects. "Did the three of you catch up with Ace and Dylan?"

"We looked for them but were told they were doing a meet-and-greet."

Logan rolled his eyes. "Typical Ace. Always acting like he's famous or something."

Julien chuckled but shook his head. "I saw them while I was setting up, but that was it, other than on the stage. We'll have to give them a call when we get home. Let them know to visit next time they're in town."

"He said something about summer. So maybe then."

"Definitely."

As we made our way up the main thoroughfare, I noticed several people still skating around the makeshift ice rink, and as we passed by, Robbie asked, "Did you get to ice-skate tonight? Priest and I did."

"Robert..."

"You did?" Julien said.

"Mhmm, earlier. When you were getting things ready."

We all stopped dead in our tracks, and Julien turned to face his husbands. "You talked *Priest* into ice skating? I don't believe it."

Robbie's eyes lit up with glee as he fished his phone out of his pocket. "I have proof!"

"Robert, we talked about this." Priest's tone was downright serious, but the no-nonsense expression had little to no effect on Robbie.

"No, you threatened me, and I'm choosing to believe you love me too much to actually kill me if I show them."

"I want to see," Julien said, holding out his hand.

"I swear, Robert. If you hand that phone over—"

A second later, Julien had the phone. The delighted laugh that followed told us that Priest was indeed caught on film ice-skating, and whatever else was there was so out of place it was making the usually serious lawyer bristle.

"Give it back, Julien."

"*Non*, this is too cute, Joel. Look at you."

"Oh, this I've got to see." Logan stepped forward, but Priest quickly blocked him.

"Not on your life."

"Okay, how about on his?" Logan said, pointing at Robbie. "I mean, you did already threaten it."

When Priest merely glared, Logan shrugged. "Eh, that's okay." He then turned and leaned into Robbie. "How about you just sit near me on the way back tomorrow? Distract me from my fear of flying."

Robbie laughed. "Deal."

We continued on to the main road, and I took Logan's

hand in an effort to keep him out of trouble. When we got to the curb, we quickly spotted our car, and Priest said, "There's no way in hell you're going to see that video, Mitchell."

"Wanna make a bet?"

"You're not funny, you know that?"

"I know. But I bet you are on ice skates. See you three tomorrow."

I opened the car door and ushered Logan inside. "Get in there, would you, troublemaker."

Robbie and Julien waved at Logan while Priest scowled, and as I said my goodbyes and slid into the back seat with Logan, I shook my head.

"You had way too much fun with that."

Logan took my face in his hands and kissed me until I'd forgotten what I was talking about. "I did, but come on, Priest on ice skates? That's too much to pass up."

"Admit it, you enjoyed this weekend, didn't you?"

Logan nipped at my lower lip and nodded. "I did. I'm going to enjoy it even more when I get you back to the hotel room."

"Hmm. I like the sound of that." I kissed him again, a little harder this time. "Merry Christmas, Mr. Mitchell."

"And a merry Christmas to *you*, Mr. Mitchell."

DYLAN

$\mathcal{A}$CE PULLED HIS Lamborghini into the drive, and as the gates shut behind us, I reached across the console and took his hand in mine.

Tonight had been a huge success, millions of dollars had been raised, and by this time next week, many of those who were in desperate need of help would be getting some of the assistance they needed. It wouldn't take care of all of the problems these organizations faced, but knowing we'd helped contribute in some way made me feel a sense of purpose—especially at this time of the year.

I rested my head back against the car seat and looked over at my handsome husband. Ace was one of the most generous people I knew. Not only with his money, but with his time, his life, himself in general. People wanted so much from the man they knew on the screen, and every time he made someone's day by smiling their way, I fell in love with him a little more.

"This weekend was wonderful," I said into the dark interior.

Ace pulled the car to a stop and turned to face me. "It was, wasn't it?"

"Mhmm. Great to catch up with friends and then do something fun that will help people who really need it."

"Agreed. And even though it was touch and go there for a while, I thought it all came together well in the end."

I smiled, thinking of the blackout and then what had followed. "I think it's safe to say it worked out *better* than well in the end. I don't think there's been such a public engagement of celebrities since you."

Ace lifted my hand to his lips and pressed a kiss to the back of my knuckles. "Since *us*, you mean."

"We did make a statement, didn't we?"

"We sure did, Daydream. I like to think that maybe we

somehow gave Viper a hand tonight. You know, to be able to put it all out there in front of the world."

I liked that thought too. "I'm happy for them. It's clear they're mad about one another. I thought their bandmates were going to pass out in shock. Viper was quite the player before Halo came along."

"So was Logan before Tate. It's amazing what the right man can do to you."

I turned Ace's hand over and rubbed my thumb over the back of his hand. "Want to know what this man is going to do to you?"

"Hell yes I do."

I reached over and pressed the release on Ace's seatbelt, and when it retracted, I placed my hand on his chest and brushed my lips over his. "I'm going to take you inside…"

"Hmmm?"

"Lay you out in bed…"

"Oh, I like this."

I grinned and moved my lips up by his ear. "And suck your big candy cane."

Ace started to laugh, a rumble of joy vibrating out of him as his wide shoulders shook.

"My candy cane, huh? That's what we're going to call it from now on?"

I sat back on my side of the car and reached for the handle. "Would you rather Santa's pole?"

Ace's mouth fell open, and I couldn't stop laughing as I pushed open the door and climbed out. Then I turned around and leaned down to see him sitting exactly where I'd left him.

"Whatcha waiting for, Hotshot? This boy's got a sweet tooth, so get your fine ass out of this car and upstairs."

Ace's smile was packed full of sex, and when he finally walked around the front of the car and we headed toward the front door, he said, "You are definitely going on the naughty list this year."

I chuckled and kissed Ace's cheek. "As long as you're there with me, I don't much care."

"Then let's go. I've got a big candy cane with your name on it, and I *really* want to give it to you."

Laughing, we made our way inside and up to our room hand in hand. There, we fell into each other's arms and reconnected in a way that was made extra special at this time of the year.

Love, laughter, friendship, and cheer—this weekend had been full of all of those things, and tonight in an arena full of strangers, we'd shared a moment in time that would help the less fortunate. I couldn't think of anything more fitting for this time of the year than reaching out and giving to my fellow man.

And speaking of my fellow man, it was time I got to work and landed the both of us firmly on that naughty list.

Thank you so much for reading *Jingle Bell Rock*. We hope you enjoyed reconnecting with some of our most beloved characters.

If you'd like to catch up with their individual stories you can find them at the links below!

Logan & Tate (Temptation Series)
Ace & Dylan (Preslocke Series)
Viper & Halo (Fallen Angel Series)
Robbie, Julien, & Priest (Confessions Series)
Panther & Solo (Elite Series)
Shaw & Trent (South Haven Series)
Paige & Dawson w/Ryleigh (LA Liaisons Series)

Stay well and safe, and let's make 2021 an EPIC year (in a good way)!!

**Love Jingle Bell Rock? Leave a review!*
Reviews are vital to authors, and all reviews, even just a couple of quick sentences, can help a reader decide whether to pick up our books.
*If you enjoyed this book, please consider leaving a review on the site you purchased from.**

Brooke Blaine is a *USA Today* Bestselling Author of contemporary and LGBT romance that ranges from comedy to suspense to erotic. The latter has scarred her conservative Southern family for life, bless their hearts.

If you'd like to get in touch with her, she's easy to find - just keep an ear out for the Rick Astley ringtone that's dominated her cell phone for years. Or you can reach her at www.BrookeBlaine.com.

Brooke's Links
Brooke's Newsletter
Brooke & Ella's Naughty Umbrella

www.BrookeBlaine.com
brooke@brookeblaine.com